I0753534

FINISHING LINE PRESS
www.finishinglinepress.com

Hair Brush with Fame

My painfully awkward life amid the big wigs

by

Lisa Johnson Mitchell

Finishing Line Press
Georgetown, Kentucky

Hair Brush with Fame

My painfully awkward life amid the big wigs

ISBN 979-8-89990-459-2 First Edition

ACKNOWLEDGMENTS

To my beloved family for all their support and patience,
as I told and retold these stories ad nauseum.
To my brilliant colleague, Karen Scamardo, who helped me perfect the title.
To Deven Fulton for the sassy book cover design.
To Lucas Buckels for technical (and emotional) support.
To Gabby Covey for being my inimitable copyeditor.
And to all the celebrities who gave me my moment in the sun.

Publisher: Leah Huete de Maines
Editor: Christen Kincaid
Cover Art: iStock/TOBKATRINA
Author Photo: Hal Samples
Interior Photos: Lisa Johnson Mitchell
Cover Design: Elizabeth Maines McCleavy

Order online: www.finishinglinepress.com
also available on amazon.com

Author inquiries and mail orders:
Finishing Line Press
PO Box 1626
Georgetown, Kentucky 40324
USA

Contents

For my beloved parents, John and Phyllis.

Introduction

My dad did hair. Ladies came to him to get their hair "done." If you're from the South, you know what this means. The name of his salon was Preston Hairdressers. It was in Park Cities, the Beverly Hills of Dallas. The heyday of this magical place was during the 1960s-70s, when big hair was big business in Texas.

Along with school teachers, church members, and SMU sorority girls, the customers included some of Dallas' most famous: the former mayor, Annette Strauss. The real estate icon, Ebby Halliday. *Dallas Morning News* editor and author, Lee Cullum. Finally, Lulu Roman, the star of *Hee Haw,* and be still my heart, Carol Burnett!

For some mystical reason—perhaps it was growing up in this fanciful, glittery milieu—I have found myself popping up time after time in the company of the famous, from John Malkovich to Russell Crowe to Prince Albert of Monaco, to name a few. And doing so in the most bizarre, awkward of ways.

These are my stories.

1973. The Butt Cut Laura Ingalls Wilder
aka Little House on the Prairie.

Me and Lulu from *Hee Haw*

God tapped me on the shoulder one night.

I was about four and in bed. Suddenly, I felt a couple of pokes on my shoulder. Huge inhale. I froze. Finally, I turned over to see who it was. No one was there, but I knew it was My Maker.

When I was six, I told my mother I could see the air. I saw little squiggles, grey amoebas swimming around, interlocked like lace, pulsing like my heart, vibrating in my soul.

As I recalled these two mystical, inexplicable events, there emerged from the mist of my memory a person who tied up my childhood celestial imaginings in a neat, nice bow. She brought it all together as a beacon of meaning—someone who was sent from above to give me a message.

Through the haze in my mind, she was standing behind the receptionist desk inside Dad's beauty salon. She leaned over, grasped my upturned hand, and read my palm. She told me what my astrological chart said about me, what my 13-year-old self could expect in the years to come.

The woman? Lulu Roman, star of *Hee Haw*, a vivacious, perky gal with a sweet smile you could just fall into. She held my hand gingerly like it was a pearl. Her hands were soft, but firm. Her soul was overflowing, generous. She had oceans to share. I waited with high hopes about what she would tell me about my life.

"You are very important." Her eyes gleamed with light and hope. "You will do big, important things in your life. You have a reason to be here. When you were born, you had all your planets in the House of Theater. This means," she said with a delicate, short breath, "you have a voice that must be heard."

She had given me my mission—my marching orders from the universe.

Lulu was not the receptionist at Dad's salon—she was just filling in for my grandmother who usually "worked the desk." She was married to Woody Smith, one of Dad's "operators." That's the word he used to describe his employees, the hairdressers who worked for him.

(Last I heard of Woody and Lulu, they'd divorced, and he'd moved to Branson. Rumor had it that there were a lot of retirement homes from all over the country that took excursions to this Country Vegas Amusement Park. Woody's specialty was back-combing, teasing, and coifs. The ladies loved him and he, them.)

Lulu's proclamation of the trajectory of my life went in and out of my mind for years. Her long career as a comedian and entertainer, and her larger-than-life persona, hung in my heart, as did her prediction for my life's path.

I hadn't looked into Lulu for years, until I recently Googled her, and discovered that she'd passed away.

What an impressive life she'd led. Her website had a list of her accomplishments and awards that were seemingly never-ending. Here are a few, starting with the most-recognized:

- 1968-1995—Regular cast member on *Hee Haw.*
- 1980—Guest performer at President Ronald Reagan's inauguration.
- 1999—Inducted into the Country Gospel Music Hall of Fame.
- 2008—Inducted into the Christian Music Hall of Fame.

In addition to her fame, what seemed the most miraculous was her total and utter transformation. Over the years, she'd reinvented herself and lost 200 pounds.

I, too, have transformed through the years. I performed my story, my Soul on Parade, at the Wyly Theatre in downtown Dallas in a storytelling show titled "Ducks in a Row," part of, *Oral Fixation,* a show akin to *The Moth* in New York City.

In my eight-minute piece, I detail the irony of pulling out all my hair and having a hairdresser for a father. That, and my crazy journey through corrective shoes, sneaking boys into my room as a teenager, OCD, anxiety in Manhattan, and finally, freedom in sobriety.

I'm still searching for the meaning of my childhood intersection with the iconic Lulu in Dad's beauty salon. Is it that I love to laugh, love to "hee haw" and have a good ol' time? That if asked to choose between sex and laughter, it would be a big toss-up? That my wish to shed my "thirty pounds of life" can be a reality?

Truth is, I have no final answer to any of this, like on that *Millionaire* show. But the true piece of info I can impart is that my story is still unfolding. My mission is still in play.

1977. The Feathered Farrah Fawcett.

Olivia Newton-Johnson

During high school, the church was my second home. I lived, breathed, and ate church. I was in the youth group, and I also sang in the youth choir called The Variations, a clever name derived from the wide variety of musical numbers we would perform each year, as well as a neat little pun out of the music lexicon.

As a Variations member, I wore a cherry-red polyester leisure suit that had a matching polyester shirt, replete with ginormous lapels. The shirt was white, and on it was a scattering of little red and blue shapes akin to PAC MAN—kind of early emoticons.

We sang at churches, old folks' homes, burn centers, and orphanages. Our repertoire consisted of Christian youth musicals like *Celebrate Life, Tell it Like it Is,* and *Lightshine*, each with distinct, jazz-hand centric choreography, square-dancing moves, kick lines, and snappy contagions. One time we performed a three-part round that kicked off one of the musicals. It consisted of our running down the aisles in succession in three groups, our hands flailing about our heads as if the church was on fire, hollering at the top of our lungs: "HE is alive, he IS alive, he is ALIVE."

The entire congregation was terrified.

The Variations toured every summer. We went to exotic places like Texarkana, Baton Rouge, and one fated summer evening, San Antonio. We performed at an orphanage—the very same night Olivia Newton-John was in town for a concert.

After our dinner, the choir collectively decided we'd take a boat ride down the river, one that cut through the shopping and dining area called the Riverwalk.

Since the boats were not that big and couldn't carry all of us, we broke up into groups. I got on the boat with my buddies, as well as our senior pastor, Dr. Ben Oliphint.

About midway through the boat ride, Dr. Oliphint let out one of his signature siren sounds. Yes, he would howl from the depth of his lungs this noise that sounded exactly like a fire engine coming down the road. He could've made a lot of money as a Foley artist in Hollywood.

As he was letting out this deafening siren blast, he then yells out, "Olivia Newton-John ... Olivia Newton-JOHN, everybody ... RIGHT HERE," at which point he said, "Stand up, Lisa, and start waving."

Now, in addition to the enormous lapels on my shirt that flapped in the breeze, I also had a big, frosted blond Farrah Fawcett hairdo with Texas-size wings that flapped in the wind right along with my lapels. At that time, Olivia and I had remarkably similar hair.

From a distance, I looked the part. I was her body double, her doppelganger. This was my chance to put my youth choir performing chops to the test.

I stood up and started waving. Suddenly, people started waving back, and some started running down the Riverwalk with cameras, snapping photos.

The lights flashed one after the other. Click, click, click! It was a paparazzi fest. The farther we sailed, the bigger the crowds got. Large

My photo taken by Sally Hill somewhere in the Park Cities.

groups of my "fans" started running down each side of the riverbank, snapping more photos and shouting, "Olivia! Olivia!"

The more adulation I got, the more I waved.

We sailed on a bit more and I sat down. The ruse had run its course. Everyone on our boat had a good laugh.

As we docked, I prayed that no one would come up to me and give me a frowny face for not being Olivia.

But then, just after I got off the boat and walked into a restaurant, a little girl came up to me. With her big, brown puppy dog eyes, she took my hand and looked up at me.

"Are you really Olivia Newton-John?"

My heart just broke. I just couldn't continue the joke. "No, I'm not."

Her face dropped right to the ground, and I could feel her disappointment in my bones.

Her mother came up to fetch her. We both smiled and she grabbed her daughter's hand, gave me a look of silent disapproval, and led her away.

So, what's the moral of this story? First, it's a testament to the fact that the cult of celebrity does seem to get a crowd all stirred up. Why? Because it's as if when we get to touch the hem of their garment, we'll be healed, or blessed. God-like.

Case in point: I was on a shoot in the '90s in Los Angeles, and Michael Jackson was shooting a music video right next door to us.

We all had our eagle eyes out to catch a glimpse of him. During a break, we saw Michael Jackson emerge from his trailer, but it was from a distance. He was wearing his signature surgical mask. (He was a germophobe, a known OCD sufferer, so no surprise. I felt an immediate kinship.)

We were all amped up—abuzz. We'd seen him: Michael Jackson! We had chills—big adrenaline rush. We all walked just a little taller back onto the set, bragging to the crew about our sighting.

Later, we found out that it was his body double. I think I knew, perhaps, how that little girl in San Antonio felt. It was a buzzkill, a letdown, for sure. That feel-good extra specialness, that a-little-bit-better-than feeling escaped, like a just-popped helium balloon.

But such is life. Many of us live ordinary lives sans celebrity, our "quiet lives of desperation," to quote Thoreau. Dad used that quote from time to time. I think he felt that way, desperate, because he felt he hadn't lived up to his potential by only owning a small business and never lived his dream of going to law school.

He died in 2003 and to this day, he's still my hero. That's why in his honor, I try to live every day as if it were my last. It squashes the desperation right out of my soul.

This is the star-turn I live for.

Many years after the whole Riverwalk event, from time to time, I'd think about that little girl. Should I have lied to her? Would that have been better than disappointing her? I honestly don't know. What tipped me toward telling the truth was, well, truth. No matter how painful, truth is always better. At least, this is what I learned from church, the First United Methodist Church in downtown Dallas, where I was, for one brief shining moment on a river boat in San Antonio, Olivia Newton-Johnson.

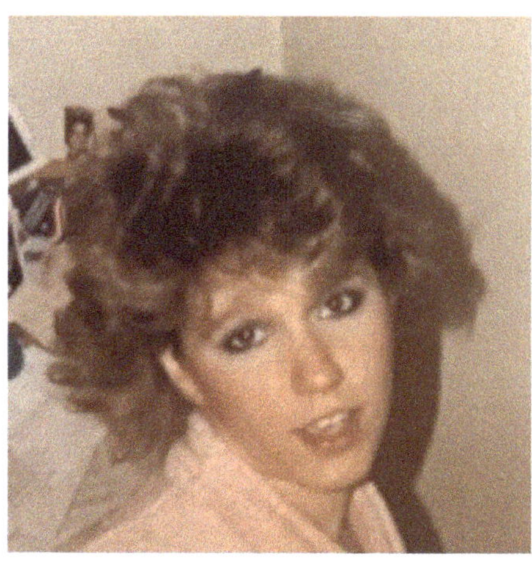

1983. The Fluffy Brown Molly Ringwald from Sixteen Candles.

Soup with the Prince

In 1982, after my summer internship at Wells, Rich, Greene in Dallas, followed by a two-week interterm at WRG in Manhattan, I graduated from Southern Methodist University (aka SMU) and jetted right back to the Big Apple—one-way ticket. I milked the connections I'd established and landed a job as a secretary in WRG's sales promotion department. I worked for Chuck Damon, a spectacled gay man with a goatee, a cute paunch, and sprayed, stiff hair. He had a staff of about eight art directors and copywriters for whom I answered phones, typed on a manual typewriter, and fetched coffee, all while attending the School of Visual Arts at night to work on my copywriting portfolio.

So here I was, public-school Lisa, working for my sorority sister's mom, Mary Wells Lawrence, at her utterly glamorous company on the twenty-eighth floor of the GM building, right across from the Plaza and Central Park. During the fall, the leaves in the park glistened in yellow, orange, and red, and from my boss' office, the view was cinema on steroids—breath-stealing. There was no fall in Dallas. The magic of Manhattan held me in its grip.

As I peered into the offices, I saw walls lined with white paper and crazy black marker jottings: headlines, designs, layouts. The bubbling-over-the-sides energy of the creatives, dressed in designer clothes—Betsey Johnson, Armani—with cigarettes in one hand and sketch pads in the other, was invigorating. I had to do this.

One day, Mary's assistant called me down to her office. Had I shown up late one too many days? Had I insulted *Gumercindo*, one of the staff from Mary's villa, Fiorentina, on the French Riviera? She brought Gumercindo, whom I called Goobercindo because he was such a fussy pants, over from Monaco to work at the agency, and he seemed to be perpetually perturbed with me.

But I was not being fired.

I was being invited to a Valentine's Day party in honor of Prince Albert of Monaco.The party was dubbed "informal." Back in those days, that meant a silk dress and pearls. The night before, I was so excited I couldn't sleep. I'd seen the young prince around the agency. Mary employed her clients' kids as summer interns, along with children of her neighbors in the South of France, where they lived part of the year. The prince was about to be a senior at Amherst. When he sailed past my secretarial station, I averted my eyes and pretended to type. I peered after him as he disappeared down the long hallway. He was usually dressed in subtle, expensive clothes. He wore glasses and was already slightly balding. Slim and sleek, like his mother, Grace Kelly.

The night before the party it snowed, so the next evening I clomped down eight flights of stairs in the apartment building—the elevator was broken—in black, patent leather Ferragamo flats I got on sale (especially slippery on the marble stairs) and waited, shivering, behind the glass-paned street door. I wore a shocking hot pink Talbots dress with a high neckline and a sash at the waist. A string of pearls (of course), thin white hose, as was the fashion back then, and a coat Dad had bought me at Neiman

Marcus' Last Call, trimmed in fake fur. My hair was blah brown but was curly and covered my bald patches—my trichotillomania, a hair-pulling form of OCD.

At 6:30 p.m. a limo finally arrived. I cautiously made my way across the arctic sidewalk. The driver hopped out and opened my door. I scooted in and sat next to State Lawrence, Harding's son. He was named "State" because of Harding's love for states' rights.

"Next stop," State said, "Park Avenue. Albert Grimaldi."

The name sounded familiar, Grimaldi: Wasn't that the name of a grocery store? Perhaps he was the heir. We rounded the corner onto Park Avenue and stopped in front of a stately doorman building. Then it clicked: It was the prince.

Albert slid in and nodded to State. The car was so quiet I could hear the two men breathing. We inched along toward the Upper East Side; the speed of our trek was glacial. I attempted to engage Albert in conversation, playing the "Do you know ________" game, as I was acquainted with some of his work buddies, but he wasn't interested. His eyes locked in on the city as it scrolled by.

When the elevator doors opened at Mary's East End penthouse, I was puzzled. There was no front door. We were right *in* the penthouse. The first thing I saw was a painting that might have been a Picasso. And there was Mary dressed like a film star in what looked to be a Givenchy gold shift, greeting and hugging everyone.

"Lisa, welcome! This is Cecelia. Cecelia, Lisa." We nodded to each other. "Will you please introduce her around the party?" Cecilia was, and still is, Gregory Peck's daughter.

Off we went, me in my blinding pink Talbot's dress, a garish neon spot bobbing in a sea of devastating black, the attire of the evening—I didn't get the memo. I finally managed to get Cecelia talking to a small group of older people and shrank away to find Pam, Mary's daughter, my only friend at the party.

I found Pam by the hors d'oeuvres, munching on some carrot sticks. Her dark eyes softened when she saw my furrowed brow. I filled her in on what had just happened.

"That's my mom," she said with a wink.

Soon we were guided into a grand room with floor-to-ceiling windows overlooking Manhattan, containing two large, round tables with white, perfectly pressed tablecloths. I was seated next to William Doyle of the famous auction house on Madison Avenue. On the other side of me was a guy who ran a Greek shipping company, who I later found out might have been Aristotle Onassis' nephew.

At each place setting were a dizzying number of utensils (too many spoons and some were placed horizontally along the top of my shiny plate) and a little blue box from Tiffany's—party favors. The men got a gold money clip, the women, a classic floating Elsa Peretti heart gold necklace.

The food was dished out with nary a spill by the white-aproned attendants from Villa Fiorentina. The first course was supposedly a French chicken soufflé, but it actually looked more like one of Mamaw's chicken pot pies.

Next, we were served bowls of clear lemon soup. I dipped my spoon in, took a small taste, and I quietly gagged. It was terrible—tart and strange—but I didn't want to be rude. As I was about to take another spoonful, I saw people putting their fingers into the soup and rubbing them together.

My face erupted into a firestorm.

A man cleared his throat. It was Goobercindo, who hovered over me. He mouthed, "Put the spoon down."

He took it out of my hand, slipped it into his pocket, and gave me a smug smile. I glanced around the table and discretely swallowed as much water and wine as I could to wash the hideous concoction from my mouth. What I really wanted was a shot (or twenty) to take away my ambient shame. Fortunately, from what I could tell, nobody had seen me drink from the finger bowl. Mary's and the prince's heads were turned, eyes fastened on each other, engaged in conversation.

After dinner, we took an elevator to another floor where Michael Feinstein, in a tuxedo, was playing show tunes on the piano. In came Goobercindo with a tray bearing after-dinner drinks and cognac—just the anesthetic I needed to quell my dinner faux pas. He returned with an assortment of chocolates and cigarettes. I imagined Goobercindo was sick of me by then, but as he was walking away, I grabbed his sleeve and whispered, "Thank you."

"But of course," he said.

When I got home, I didn't sleep that night. Being transported out of my ordinary life into this dream of conspicuous consumption spawned a hunger for things I'd never known existed, even more than it did in college. Even my skin felt different.

Here's the thing: It was so easy to invent and reinvent yourself when you lived in New York. Each day, I could step out of my apartment and become whoever I wanted to be. One day, I dressed like a preppy out of a Whit Stillman film. The next day, I might don a man's vintage coat, fedora, neon-pink socks, and ballet flats. Once, I even wore the full-length ranch mink Dad went into debt to buy me, with a pair of high-top, red Converse sneakers. I loved being a chameleon, and I would never be found out.

After that magical evening, I began spending money on things I couldn't afford: daily lunches at Bergdorf's; expensive dinners on the Upper East Side; Italian shoes in Soho. I dug myself further and further into credit card debt; however, occasionally, I got a few hundred from Mom and Dad, which barely covered a weekend of dining and dancing. Then I began winning ad awards and meeting more famous people, and drinking, drinking, drinking.

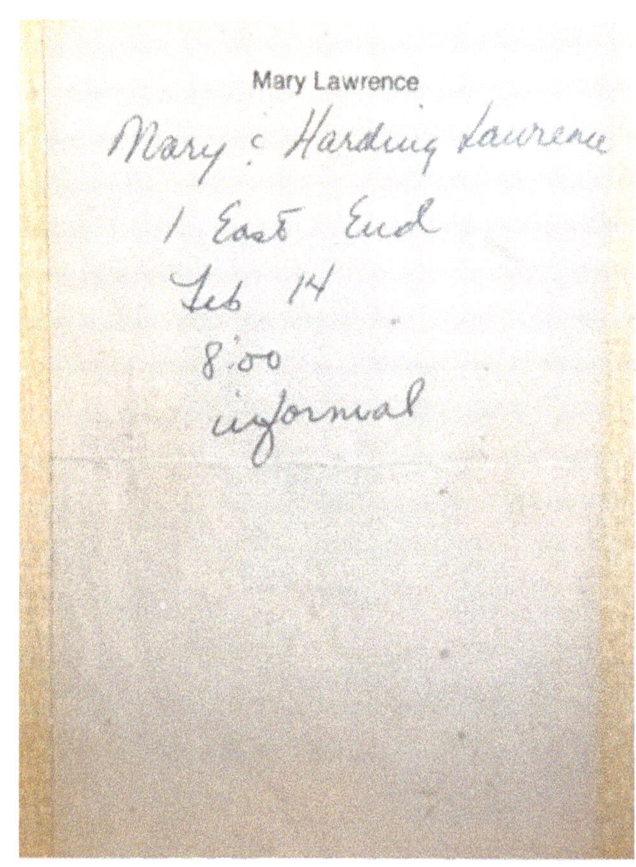

Mary Lawrence

Mary & Harding Lawrence
1 East End
Feb 14
8:00
informal

Invitation from Mary Wells Lawrence.

1984. The Bedhead Stevie Nicks (or Steven Tyler).

My Starr Turn

New York. Christmas in the mid-80s. I snagged an invitation to a toney party at a club in Midtown with my friend Henry. He'd been invited by a Hollywood producer, a guy who originally hailed from London. My boyfriend at the time seemed to be quite jealous.

The club's theme was the '60s and was adorned with vintage guitars, black and white photos of starlets and leading men, the likes of Elizabeth Taylor, Cary Grant, and John Wayne, their grainy smiles arced in immaculate crescents. I sauntered up to the bar, bought drinks, and brought them back to my group. The topic of conversation centered on a guest the producer and his wife had met while in Barbados and was the son of a Beatle, whom they'd invited to the soiree. He was standing nearby, alone, aloof, surveying the crowd. His hair, dark and straight, hung perfectly down to his waist. He was dressed in black, head to toe. I wore a Stevie Nicks inspired coif, one of my go-to black dresses, and capped it off with flats and eye-hurting neon lime socks. Being fearless after a few drinks—my liquid courage—I took a deep breath and walked up to him. I was a bit taller, but not too much.

"Hi, saw you here, thought you might be lonely. Name's Lisa." I extended two fingers.

"I'm Jason Starkey." We shook.

"Oh, no you're not. Your last name is Starr."

"But my father's name is Richard Starkey."

"No, it isn't. It's Ringo Starr."

After going back and forth like this for a bit, he convinced me who he was: Jason Starkey, son of Ringo. My neck warmed with embarrassment. So to distract him from my gaffe, a song came on—by the Beatles—and I seized the moment: I asked him to dance.

"I cahn't dance." He repeated, "I cahn't dance."

We stood frozen, me toggling between acute awkwardness and total elation, as the iconic, nasally refrain, "I want to hold your hand," bounded around us. He, however, remained the very picture of calm. I pulled him out to the dance floor, but he wasn't having it.

We grew tired of the cigarette smoke, the noise, the elbows in our backs, and he asked if I wanted to go to the Hard Rock Cafe. We grabbed a cab to 57th Street, zipped past the hideously long line, and went upstairs to meet his mother, Maureen, now divorced from Ringo and married to Isaac Tigrett, owner of the Hard Rock Cafe empire.

Maureen was dressed in all black, too. Her beautiful smoky eyes were hugged by thick, dark eyeliner. She held her cigarette in a long, slender black holder as she seemed to silently judge me. On her pointer finger was a silver skull ring. We sat down and ordered martinis, and the manager walked up—Yul Brenner's son. He made sure we were all taken care of, that the drinks were on the house. Eventually, I mentioned that I had MTV at my apartment. Jason piped up. "I want to watch the telly."

At my apartment, we tiptoed past the door of my roommate and proceeded to stay up all night propped up on the floor against my bed watching MTV. We didn't even have any coke to help us stay up; he was entranced with MTV, and I was entranced with him—until I found out he was only seventeen. I was twenty-four. He said he thought I was his age. I began to squirm.

Daylight broke and we were still up. A weirdness sluiced through my bones. I was scared, as if I'd held him hostage and the Beatles Police were going to bang on my door, demanding his release. I shooed him out and put him in a cab. He called me a few times from Martha's Vineyard, where he and his mum were staying; then they went back to London.

A year later, in August 1985, Jason called and said he was going to be in New York. I told him it was my birthday and that I would take him out to dinner. And I did, even though I didn't have the money. My sycophantic offer seemed so natural. I had a penchant for kowtowing to those of means (or fame) to gain approval.

After going to Petrosian for champagne and caviar, followed by a trendy new restaurant in Midtown, we ended up at a record store. We browsed albums by the Thompson Twins and Howard Jones. Somehow, the guy who worked there figured out who Jason was. Truth: I told him who Jason was. The next thing we knew, the record store employee was running after us, waving a cassette of his band's latest song. As we got into the cab, Jason politely took it, and said he'd share it with his dad. I dropped him at his hotel and went home.

He continued to call me for a year or so, always late at night, after he'd been out and about. We talked mostly about music and movies. His favorite singer at the time was Paul Rogers and one night, he told me he'd been to Michael Caine's house.

"I sat in his chaihr," he said. "I sat in Michael Caine's chaihr."

In 1986, Jason called and said he might be coming to Dallas for the opening of the Hard Rock. I was planning to go home for my birthday at about the same time. When I got to town, I made a beeline for the restaurant to see if he was there.

Turned out, he was—a fluke. No cell phones back then to communicate every scintilla of movements we made. We enjoyed a few strong drinks at the bar. I got a tad wasted, then switched to soda that only mildly helped and started petting his long, luscious midnight black hair, which was interrupted by my hiccups. "You're so prehty." HICKup. "Sawry, you're so," HICup, "prehty." He didn't seem to mind.

After plowing through burgers and fries, an attempt to sober up, I got the bright idea of giving him a tour of Dallas, which included a Lisa Retrospective. I was driving Dad's brown 1975 Peugeot. It had a few dents, but at night they were negligible.

About 2 a.m., as we approached my high school hangout, The Hill, a parking lot that overlooked White Rock Lake, the car began to make weird noises and finally died. But I knew how to start it up. Someone had to get out and push it while someone else turned the ignition key.

"Can you help me?"

"Right-o." And he hopped out.

There I was, with the son of Ringo Starr, who was pushing my car and running, as I turned the key, his Beatle boots slipping on the pavement, in Dallas, Texas. How had my life gotten to this point?

A few years later, Mom and I went to Scotland—I'd won a trip (for two) after T. Boone Pickens picked my name out of a hat at the Women's Service League luncheon—and stopped off in London. I called Jason's number, and a stern voice came on the answering machine and said that if you didn't have any real business calling, you better hang up.

I never asked Jason about Ringo, though he did bring him up occasionally. I knew he must have been living in his father's shadow. And that probably didn't feel very good. Certainly, he had a different dynamic than I did. I hid my Dad's profession. In a macho, beer-drinking, football-obsessed Texas world, I was often made fun of, bullied. But I loved him madly, regardless.

Jason couldn't hide like me. His dad was Ringo Starr. I'm sure he broadcasted it any time he could. My Dad did hair. I kept it under my hat tucked away. But ultimately, I realized we had something in common: We were twin children of different fathers.

Photo of Jason Starkey and Robert Plant, Jason's prized possession he gave to me.

1986. The Dirty Dancing *Jennifer Grey.*

My Della Femina Debut

"From Those Wonderful Folks Who Brought You Pearl Harbor."

Tagline suggested by Jerry Della Femina for a prominent Japanese car company.

Yes, you read it right. This was what Jerry had suggested in a meeting full of top executives from Japan. Or so the legend goes. This shocking verbiage was also the name of Jerry's best-selling, hilarious book. Equally provocative was the subhead, which read *Front Line Dispatches from the Advertising War.* It was a war. And I was in the trenches. Even though it was 1983, Della Femina, Travisano and Partners, the hallowed, revered Madison Avenue ad agency that birthed the Creative Revolution in the '60s, was still in full, uproarious swing.

Mad Men, step aside. Back away from your egos. This was the real deal. And my very first job as an ad copywriter.

I was fresh out of *The Bubble*, SMU in the Park Cities in Dallas, Texas, where I'd been sheltered and coddled by a society and ecosystem that was a breeding ground for a big nest of WASPS.

And here I was, smack dab in the middle of the New York ad world working for a witty provocateur who also famously said, "Advertising was the most fun you could have with your clothes on." Oh, and did we.

In those days, we were allowed to smoke (#guilty) in our offices, and cocktails were shaken and stirred for any reason, or no reason at all. I mean, who needed one? It was a *partay* waiting to happen, at any given moment, on any given day. It was an odd, endlessly exciting world, one unlike any other I had ever encountered. Actually, it was more like an adult playpen. Extended adolescence. But a place, nevertheless, where magic happened.

My colleagues sported exotic names like Frank DiGiacomo. Joe Della Femina. Phil Silvestri. Mark Yustein. And Karee Rubenstein. Lots of Italians and Jews—everyone dark and swarthy all around me. Then there was pale-faced me, Lisa Johnson, or Junior Miss, Miss Texas, and any of the other nicknames they lovingly called me.

In any event, there I was, Sue Vanilla (#whitebread) trying to stay afloat amidst this colorful crew, daily standing back in awe watching them create killer ads effortlessly. To top it off, I was one of two female writers at this famous boys' club. Despite the fact that I tried to dress the part of a New York copywriter by doing the whole antique-boutique, vintage thing, Della Femina was still a lot to take in for this little Dallas girl with frosted blond hair (#thanksdad).

I wasn't good at what I did back then. No creative muscle to speak of. While I was good at puns, and was the ultimate *punographer*, ad concepts I just couldn't generate. I'd gone to the School of Visual Arts and taken portfolio classes. I cobbled together a "book," a model's portfolio full of my speculative—"spec"—ads drawn on typing paper with Marks-A-Lots. I got the job, which to me was a miracle. But at this point, I was painfully slow and needed remedial help. I had no Concepting Legs; I could've used a walker.

In addition to "ideating" and "papering the walls with layouts," as we used to say, the offices were always abuzz with lots of hollering and laughing and yucking it up, until 5 p.m., at which point on Fridays, it was time for a bit of liquid inspiration. The location: the bar in Frank's office, where he had a little fridge full of wine and beer, as well as a small table with all kinds of other liquors and libations.

As the only Junior Copywriter in the bunch, I was chronically afraid to go into this gathering of seasoned pros; they'd won every award you can name (#Cannes #OneShow #Clio). Though one afternoon, I had to venture in. After I'd slaved away for hours coming up with just the right headline, I wanted to get my supervisor's approval.

As I sucked up my courage to walk in, I approached Mark (#princeofaguy), and said, sheepishly, "Hi, can I get you to look at this?"

He looked over his glasses, cocktail in hand, and smiled. "Lisa, this is cocktail hour. We'll look at that tomorrow."

I need to add that Mark Yustein was an ad god. As an art director, he was part of the team that came up with the famous line for Meow Mix, "Tastes so good, cats ask for it by name." He also partnered with several writers to pen the brilliant Blue Nun wine radio commercials featuring the inimitable banter between Jerry Stiller and Ann Meara.

I was surrounded by greatness. So, it was only natural that during this time in my life, I was a bit more serious about the ad game, staying late nearly every night, honing my craft, puffing away on Marlboro Reds, and scarfing down head-sized, heart-clogging pretzels with mustard for dinner.

One day I was rather distraught. The client had changed one of my headlines for a newspaper ad. I marched into Ron Travisano's office simply beside myself. How could this have happened? What was the client thinking?

Ron tried to calm me down, but I just couldn't be consoled. Finally, he said, "Lisa, get ahold of yourself. People use these to line the bottom of their bird cages. Relax. This is only an ad." Boy, did that hit me like a Mack truck. WHAT? You can't be serious. I was in this for blood—and awards! And an award I got with the help of Senior Writer Rita Senders—I was a Clio Finalist, complete with an invitation to the ceremony at the Waldorf. I still have the menu from lunch that day, and on it, a nice dime-sized stain of champagne vinaigrette.

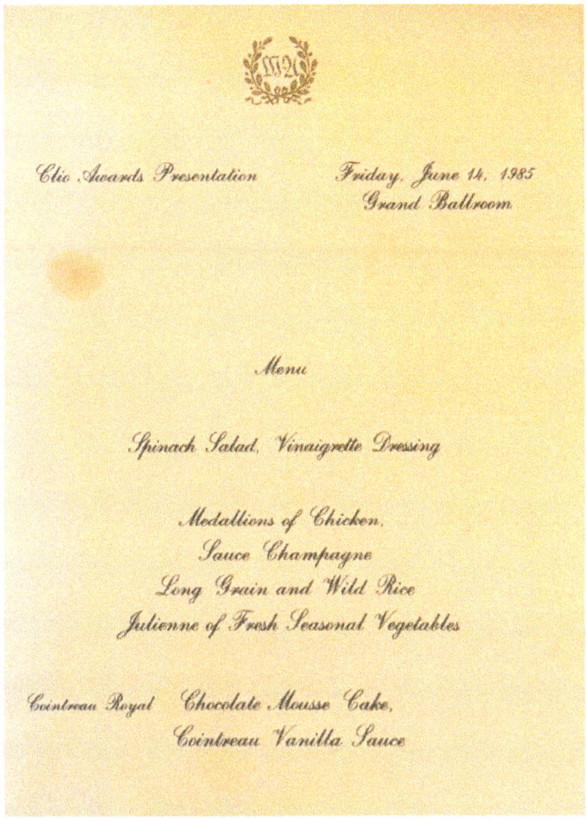

Clio Awards Presentation

Friday, June 14, 1985
Grand Ballroom

Menu

Spinach Salad, Vinaigrette Dressing

Medallions of Chicken,
Sauce Champagne
Long Grain and Wild Rice
Julienne of Fresh Seasonal Vegetables

Cointreau Royal *Chocolate Mousse Cake,*
Cointreau Vanilla Sauce

Clio luncheon menu with dime-sized dollop of dressing.

Even though Jerry was the head guy, he was frequently out of the office, rustling up new business, I'm sure. I didn't present work to him (thankfully), but one day, I had to. My bosses were out on a shoot. His assistant set up some time for me to see him.

Nervous, fidgety, overly-apologetic, and scared as a little church mouse,

I sat across from epic greatness in the form of Jerry Della Femina. Clad in his sleek Italian finery with the top of his iconic hairless head gleaming in the fluorescent lights above, he smiled and looked at me over the top of his glasses. "Have a seat, my dear."

We were working on an ad for *The New York Times* for First Boston, an investment bank. I struggled with what to say in the headline. I didn't do math or numbers, much less banking. But I did come up with a nugget of an idea. I presented it, we lobbed it back and forth a few times, then we birthed: "What every great banker needs is a great banker."

Oh, what a feeling! (Cue the *Flashdance* anthem.)

I was titillated, energized, but also relieved that my meeting with him was over and I was no longer in his office. He was just too much for me in my meager twenty-three years of life and my yet-to-be-fully-developed frontal lobe.

The only other time I really got a good chance to see Jerry, other than when I saw him in Frank's office deep into storyboards, was when he walked down the hallway one day playing the ukulele. It was a joyous sight to behold.

Another fun event was when the office was getting redecorated. For some reason, after the walls had been stripped bare of wallpaper, we created a contest involving toilet paper rolls. Whoever could stack them up next to their doors in the most creative way got a prize, which I think was a hot dog.

But it wasn't always so magical.

I was working on a radio spot for Six Flags Great Adventure, a :30 spot. Problem was, it was coming in at :40, according to the account guy. I took another pass at shortening it and thought it was fine. In the days before email, I'd place the copy that I typed on a typewriter (#fossil) in the chair of the designated AE (account executive.) Then he/she would read it and walk it back over to my office.

On my way to lunch, I dropped the radio copy off with the AE, sure I'd nailed it. I can't remember his name. Let's call him Fred. When I got back, what appeared at my door was an irritated, red-faced, spectacled Fred fiddling with his police/porn mustache and puffing on a cigarette with an inch-long ash. "Um, Lisa. This is not working. You've got exactly thirty minutes to make this thirty seconds," at which point he hurled a stopwatch at me, narrowly missing my nose, skittering, and clanging across my glass-topped desk, knocking over my pencil holder. He stood there, swaying to and fro like a buoy in the Connecticut Sound. I could smell him six feet away. Apparently, he had just returned from a sixteen-martini lunch.

After he staggered away, I burst into tears and sulked my way into Mark's office, sniffling and trying to speak, barely able to eke out what happened. After I explained the situation, Mark was not happy. Fred got into big trouble. I hate to say it, but I was happy.

The other moment that stands out was the Christmas party at the River Café in Brooklyn. The lights of Manhattan twinkled on the East River as we partied and danced the night away.

While at Della Femina, I also had the distinct privilege of working for Luke Sullivan who penned *Hey Whipple, Squeeze This*. He was later inducted into the Copywriter Hall of Fame. I learned a tremendous amount about ad writing (and life) from him.

At one point, EST was *The Big Thing*. EST stood for Erhard Seminar Training. Everyone in the office was doing it, except me. It was rumored that they locked you in an auditorium full of strangers for an entire couple of weekends and wouldn't let you out to go to the bathroom or wear a watch, all the while pummeling you with data, shouting at you with depressing facts about humanity that eventually wore you down to a nub. Then on the last day, you were supposedly rid of all your painful childhood memories, limiting beliefs, and were built back up—made all new and pretty, rarin' and ready to change the course of your life.

The last phenomenon around the office I remember was The Hunger Project. Sounds good, right? Like you'd be helping the world, right? Well, I went to a meeting after work one night, along with Richard (my best friend) and some other folks from the agency. Jerry even went. During the evening, we were presented with staggering, heartbreaking facts about hunger along with sad faces of precious children. I wept through much of it.

We were bright-eyed and interested for the first part, but after a while, the whole presentation started to drag on and on—way too much information. About halfway through, we saw Jerry get up and leave. I leaned over and whispered to Richard, "He's probably like, 'Let's get outta here. All this talk about hunger is making me hungry. I am dying for a big plate of spaghetti.'" We could hardly contain ourselves after that.

The sad truth about The Hunger Project was that while the overall purpose of the movement was admirable, they were criticized for using most of the money for educating the public about worldwide hunger rather than actually feeding people.

But after all of these kooky happenings, the most fun, most insane, most deliriously zany event at the agency was The Sex Contest.

No, it wasn't a live sex show. But the vibe of the whole thing was deliciously wild and racy. Women voted for the man they'd most like to have sex with, and men voted for the women they'd most like to boink. The winning couple would be announced at a luncheon called The Secretaries Luncheon. The prize: a weekend at the Plaza, compliments of the agency. Beyond fabulous, right? But here's the thing: Each winner would *not* be getting their own room. The prize was one room—that the two lucky winners would share to ostensibly get lucky. Second prize was a night on Ron's couch with Virginia, our cleaning lady. The ménage à trois winners won a dinner for three at the Four Seasons. The gay winners won a $250 gift certificate for The Pleasure Chest.

The day arrived for the luncheon and the announcement of the winning couple. We shut down at noon on Friday, and all headed over to a Mexican restaurant on the Upper East Side, one we'd rented out for this soon-to-be-raucous party.

The afternoon was somewhat of a blur. All I remember is that after the winners were announced—they were both way too sexy for their shirts—the margaritas and funny cigarettes (#maryjane) started flowing. Secretaries were sitting on top of the laps of the wasted account guys as well as some handsy creative directors. I crawled out of there at some point, blotto and bleary-eyed, and went to bed for what might have been the entire weekend. Oh yeah, it was some party, the memory of which is both vague and achingly specific in my mind. Some things that happened there, I'll never share.

Lots of stuff happened during my stint at Della Femina. Decades later, Jerry was a consultant for *Mad Men*. Can't make this stuff up. Truth is always more original than fiction.

That year was one of the best of my professional life. I can honestly say it was a balls-to-the-wall year of true *Mad Men*–revelry that glows, sings, and snap-crackle-pops in my memory.

1985. The Makeshift Madonna.

The Top 2%

In 1986, I was working at Ogilvy & Mather, a storied ad agency on Madison Avenue during the glorious insanity of ’80s Manhattan—Madonna-rising, Andy Warhol–at-Studio-54 swan song, dirty, urine-soaked subways, and the heyday of Pyramid, Area, and Limelight nightclubs, where you’d see everything from a ferret on a leash to JFK, Jr.

In our Midtown office, I sat in a dingy interior hallway sandwiched between the agency producer Paul Dewey (of “Dewey Defeats Truman” fame) and Reggie Hudlin, of the filmmaking Hudlin Brothers who would go on to write *House Party*. Back then, he was on a summer internship from Harvard and had already appeared in Spike Lee’s film *She’s Got to Have It*.

One evening, Paul asked me to join a group of his friends for drinks. Among them was a handsome guy named Peter, a Duke graduate who was working at a magazine, *Manhattan, Inc*. We hit it off and dated, even spent my twenty-sixth birthday at his grandmother’s compound in Nantucket, skinny dipping during the day, cavorting between her cottages, and drinking champagne in knobby sweaters by a toasty fire at night. We ran with a crowd straight out of the movie *Metropolitan*. Everyone was boarding-school educated and destined for a life among the top 2%. And there I was, the public-school townie with my size 10 Texas feet trailing along after them.

Peter and I joined his frat brothers at a TriBeCa cafe. The dinner conversation revolved around their fraternity antics at Duke. This glistening evening was burgeoning with bespoke jackets and expensive aftershave, blushing affection—you're awesome, man!—and loving *fuck-yous,* loosened neckties, sweaty brows, women looking slyly into their compacts to apply lip gloss, their Tiffany bracelets jangling, toasts to a raise at work, an ad award won, as well as news of tickets snagged to the hottest Broadway show, a share in a coveted Hamptons summer house acquired, the death of an aunt and a huge inheritance forthcoming, the recent engagement of a playboy buddy, a promotion at an investment bank on Wall Street, and the murmurings of what after-hours place we'd go for the best Peruvian blow. That summer, I reveled in a sparkling echelon that never ceased to blow my Madonna knockoff hair back.

At one point, a dazzling blond woman sat down next to me. Her locks were straight and shiny—patrician. Superior DNA. A *Town & Country* poster child with a French manicure, clad in Clergerie sandals. She'd come with Peter's friend, Nicholas, her boyfriend. She was cordial but not too revealing. (I'm sure I'd told her my entire life story after a chardonnay or five.) She was still in college—Brown—and was in town for the weekend.

I asked if she had a cigarette. (I was not a smoker. I tried to *start* smoking for 20 years. But I never quite got it. I always burned myself or set my straw summer handbag on fire while trying to light up.) My sleek dinner companion opened her purse and retrieved a gold monogrammed cigarette case. She opened it, offered me a smoke, and I accepted. Clumsily, I stuck the chubby ciggie (I suspected they were Gitanes) in my mouth, and with one graceful click of her gilded lighter, she ignited my cancer stick.

I inhaled, though almost choked because they were so blindingly strong.

A waiter appeared with a telephone that had an excessively long, curly cord. "Miss von Bulow? Phone call."

It was Cosima von Bulow, the daughter of Claus, the billionaire from Newport who'd been accused of trying to murder his wife, Cosima's mother, Sunny. The newspapers said Cosima had sided with her father while her mom lay in an irreversible coma. Jeremy Irons starred in the movie version of this story, *Reversal of Fortune*. The Von Bulow trial dragged on for years. Claus appealed and was acquitted. I can't imagine how Cosima must have felt.

As twilight fell upon Manhattan and the lights ascended, shimmering, reflecting on the city streets, I sipped French table wine (I white-knuckled it, trying not to get blotto), dined on pomme frites, and laughed uproariously, mostly at people and things I didn't know anything about, willing my (usually) animated hands not to gravitate toward my hair.

All the while, Cosima's loyalty to and love for her father prowled in the back of my brain. How could she have seemingly abandoned her mother? I adored my beautiful Mom, but if I got honest, I understood Cosima. Despite our arguments, Dad and I were deeply connected. Still, I could've never chosen between the two. This I knew 100%.

1986. The Curly, Grown-Out Lady Di.

Captain Fiction

One afternoon in 1983, after too many mimosas at lunch, I was strolling with my best friend, Richard, down 54th Street, laughing and being conspicuously loud, when I saw a man walking toward us. He just kept walking, not veering aside as common sidewalk etiquette dictates. He was an older man, graying with distinction and dressed in what looked to be an expensive jacket, no tie.

He planted himself right in front of us—in my face. "You're a good-looking woman," he said. "You look like you'd know if a man was gay or not. Look at this." He retrieved a magazine from under his arm and flipped through the pages until his hand karate-chopped a place in the center. On the spread was a checkerboard configuration of photos showing four men with the headline "Dressed to Quill." He pointed to one of the pages showing just two men.

"Which of these guys do you think is better looking?" he said, jabbing his finger at the pages.

Who was he? Why was he asking me this? Why me?

One of the men in the photos had salt-and-pepper hair, a tweed jacket, and a mischievous smile. Behind him was a bookshelf. The other man had dark curly hair and a blank expression, was balding, wore glasses and a dark jacket. I chose this man.

"Aah, I *knew* it," the man said. He snatched the magazine out of my hands and vanished just as quickly as he'd appeared.

Richard and I looked at each other. "What just happened?"

"I have no idea," I said. "New York is bizarre."

When I returned to my office at Della Femina, I couldn't shake what had just happened. That evening, I found the magazine—it was *Esquire*—at a newsstand, thumbed through it, and realized that this mysterious man who had stopped me was the person in the spread, Gordon Lish. The other: the writer, Harold Brodkey. I had chosen Brodkey and rejected Lish, an editor.

Oh, dear God. What had I done?

I did research on Mr. Lish and was even more confounded, tied in a knot. I discovered he was not just an editor at Alfred A. Knopf and at *Esquire*, oh no, he was also known as Captain Fiction. He'd launched the careers of Raymond Carver, Cynthia Ozick, Don DeLillo, Reynolds Price, Barry Hannah, and Richard Ford. Amy Hempel had dedicated *Reasons to Live* to him.

Though I was a copywriter, I had dreams of becoming a writer beyond the advertising world—I was a whirligig of desires, trying to figure out how to escape my station in life, to do something of meaning. I enrolled in a fiction writing class at the West Side YMCA taught by the daughter of James Jones (*From Here to Eternity*), then a poetry workshop in the East Village, and finally, two playwriting classes at Playwrights Horizons and Ensemble Studio Theatre. I dubbed this my *Journey Through the Genres.*

I was a carousel of nervosa. I couldn't shake my agita for months. At this time in my life, anything could set me on a crash-and-burn course of spinning thoughts and sleepless nights.

My mind, a relentless bully, birthed a loop of passages, beginnings, and endings, of a letter that was a story of our sidewalk meeting. I wrote, wrote, and rewrote it. I was manic. (Even had unexplainable leg pains, which I discovered years later was a symptom of OCD.)

"It was you I should have chosen in the spread," I wrote, "but my sight was obscured by your shining, in-person, dashing good looks."

I was afraid to send it. This obsession plagued me on and off for a decade. A few more decades passed, and I ended up getting an MFA at Bennington College and studied with his most famous protegee in a workshop, Amy Hempel. She and Jill McCorkle influenced many of the short stories in my collection, *So as Not to Die Alone*, published in 2024 by Finishing Line Press.

However, the singular part of this story that rises above everything is what Mr. Lish told me, "You seem like you'd know if a man was gay or not."

Years later, I realized that every man I'd ever fallen in love with—and had invariably broken my heart—was gay or gay-leaning. But that's another story for another time.

In sum, a chance meeting on the street of Manhattan triggered my anxiety and obsessions, which years later led to a book. So out of my cauldron of pain, the birth of a narrative. Who'd a thunk it?

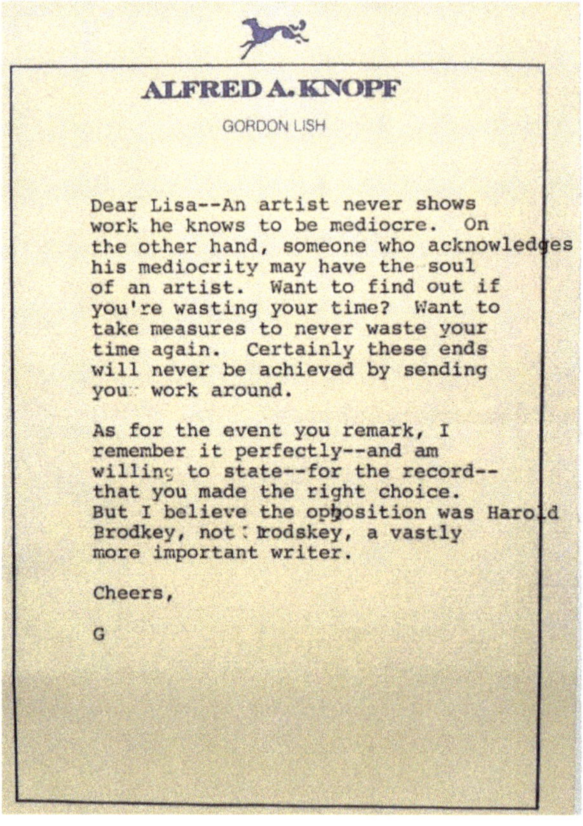

ALFRED A. KNOPF

GORDON LISH

Dear Lisa--An artist never shows work he knows to be mediocre. On the other hand, someone who acknowledges his mediocrity may have the soul of an artist. Want to find out if you're wasting your time? Want to take measures to never waste your time again. Certainly these ends will never be achieved by sending your work around.

As for the event you remark, I remember it perfectly--and am willing to state--for the record--that you made the right choice. But I believe the opposition was Harold Brodkey, not Brodskey, a vastly more important writer.

Cheers,

G

Note sent to me after I wrote to Gordon Lish about our chance meeting on the streets of New York City.

1988. The Chestnut Jami Gertz from Square Pegs.

My Afternoon with Norman

"Give me the freedom of a tightly defined strategy."

—Norman Berry, Creative Genius and Ad Legend, Ogilvy & Mather

I quote him often.

He was my big boss from 1986-89 in New York when I was a copywriter at Ogilvy & Mather.

I frequently saw him dashing by atwitter, burgeoning with disruptive, brilliant ideas, clad in Omar Sharif collared shirts inspired by *Doctor Zhivago* and made by Turnbull & Asser.

He'd be hunched over with laser-focused attention on the print ad or TV spot at hand, chain smoking, and moving his head about in bird-like sharp movements with lovely, deep, caring eyes. His laugh filled any room with hope and endless possibilities.

My assignment was for New Freedom Maxi Pads, a product from Kimberly-Clark. First, I worked on Pull-Ups, those in-between baby diapers that kids wear when they're potty training. Now it was time to move on to more mature bodily emissions: the dreaded period.

How might my partner, fabulous Senior Writer Alice Henry Whitmore and I make this interesting or most importantly, tasteful? How could we hook people and prevent them from being instantly turned off by the decidedly intimate subject matter, and change the channel the second they heard the words "maxi pad"?

We had an idea. For historical context, let's remember that this was in the late '80s. It was before the end of the Cold War. The world was a different place. People in Communist countries had little to no freedom, especially women.

For our New Freedom project, Alice and I posited a question at the top of our TV spot:

"What if the women of Moscow discovered New Freedom?"

But here's the kicker: The entire spot would be spoken in Russian—with English subtitles.

While the startlingly beautiful model we'd cast was moving freely about Red Square (love the irony), you'd hear her extolling the virtues of these awesome maxi pads that were the best thing since sliced bread (visual intended) while the translation populated the bottom of the screen:

"I can wear it everywhere I'm allowed to go. I can even wear it with my Official Party dress. I can carry them in modern pouches of plastic, even in Red Square."

And so on.

The campaign would also extend to the oppressed Chinese women and have the same opening line: "What if the women of China discovered New Freedom?"

Our lovely Chinese model would be elated about her newfangled maxis while English subtitles played on the screen.

We were tickled. We loved our idea. We thought for sure we had a big win. A smash hit, one that would march us right into the Copywriters Hall of Fame.

We couldn't wait to present this to Norman.

The day arrived for us to see him. I was terrified. Sweating. Obsessing about what to say—dashing off my notes for the setup to our brainchild, then scratching them out in a fury, and starting over again and again and again. I was a mess.

When Alice and I arrived at his office, we were surprised to see Norman sitting on the floor in front of his coffee table puffing away on a stubby, French cigarette wearing his signature Omar shirt. We sat down and joined him. I was wearing a skirt, so sitting cross-legged was not an option. Didn't want to flash anyone. I was no Sharon Stone.

I was already a bit jittery to begin with. As I positioned myself on the floor in what felt like the most awkward of poses, my leg and hip started to cramp. I thought my elbow, upon which I was leaning, was going to give way. But that all went away once we launched into our idea.

I got off to a sputtering start. "So, we thought that, well, I mean, we were thinking that, um, women in Communist countries who had few liberties would be a good juxtapose, sorry, juxtaposition to the name, New Freedom."

Luckily, Alice jumped in and saved me while she pulled out the key frames for the TV spot.

Norman inhaled his cigarette with such force, I knew we were in trouble. His brows furrowed, his eyes half shut. With an exhale like God breathing life into the universe, he said, "This is brilliant, simply brilliant. I love it. Great work, darlings."

We couldn't contain our elation. Alice and I both tried to disguise our smiles, giggled a bit, but were still focused on the work.

"However," Norman said, "this would never fly in the States."

We were heartbroken.

"It would play smashingly, swimmingly in the UK," he said. "There, you don't have the strict social mores like we have here. It would be brilliant there, but not here."

He went on. "I applaud your bold creativity, loves," he said. "Can you all come up with something else as brilliant?"

Alice and I both nodded eagerly like little cocker spaniel puppies indicating, "yes."

We thanked him for his time and floated out.

After that day, I saw him at department meetings where he'd give a rousing, encouraging speech to all and then show some stellar, recently finished spots—Seagram's Wine Cooler spots featuring Bruce Willis and Cybill Shepherd who were the stars of *Moonlighting*.

I'd even worked on the radio spot, and it was presented to Edgar Bronfman, CEO of Seagram's, with my voice recording of the spot I had written (#thrilling), but it was never bought.

Back in those days, we had an Ogilvy bar, replete with a bowtie-wearing bartender who would serve up terribly strong drinks and bowls of peanuts to the wayward, haggard account execs who needed to recover after being beaten up by the client, or weary creatives who needed to birth a new idea after theirs was savagely killed.

I loved hearing Norman give the State of the Agency address at Carnegie Hall and Radio City Music Hall, where we had our holiday meetings, after which, the Ogilvy Choir would sing. Yes, a choir filled these famous halls with lively Christmas cheer that somehow made me think of fruitcakes—the food, not the people. Also offered while I was there was a bevy of swag in Ogilvy red: watches, umbrellas, and finally, a flannel unisex nightshirt. I still have mine.

With Norman at the helm, it felt like a club. Not a company. Not a job. But a place, a home, where you could make memories, history, and lifelong friends. There was even an Ogilvy alum newsletter—way, way before social media hit. This was a place that just got things right.

In those pre–Cold War days, we could have never foretold something like Facebook. The world is radically, immeasurably different today, especially in the ad business. Mobile is King, the Grand Poobah of all. Desktop is Queen. Google is a verb.

The nerve-wracking days of meeting our air date or print deadline are mostly over. Ideas are distributed through a dizzying array of channels and are evaluated through a new lens: followers, SEO, and all those other things that make my head spin. It's a whirling dervish, a technological cauldron of activity which, if I let it, can become a time-sucking life invader.

These days, if I am in a meeting with ad folks, I'll invariably quote Norman. Sadly, few people know his classic maxim. It's too bad. It has helped me many times when explaining to a client why the TV spot filled with fifteen competing ideas just won't work.

Here's to you, Norman. My time with you was brief, but meaningful, indelibly etched on my heart. Because after all the hoopla of new media is said and done, and even after we've moved on to The Next Big Thing, you and your timeless, tightly defined words still reign.

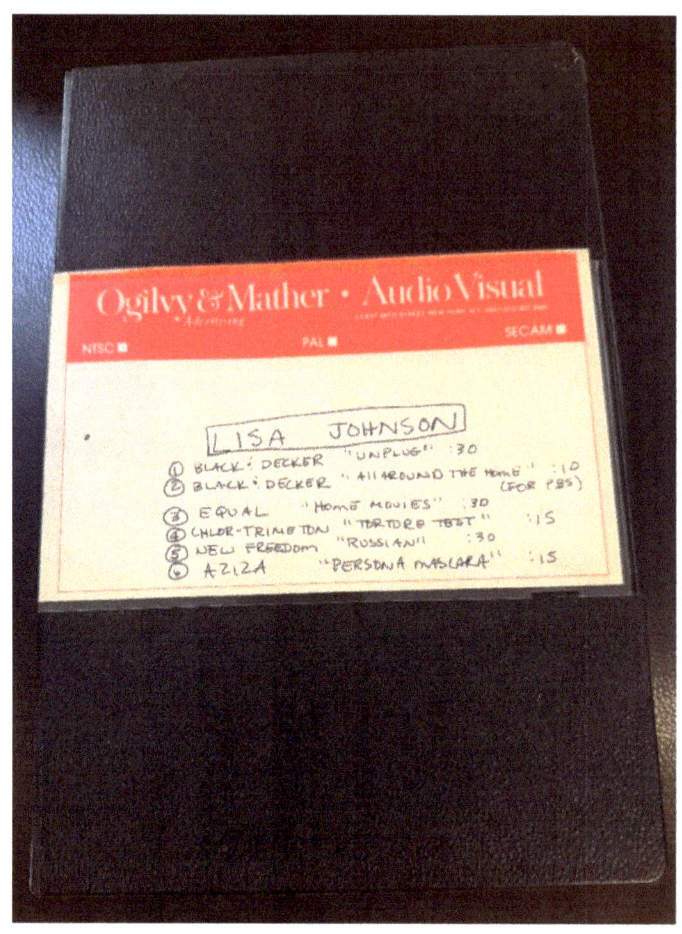

This is my "reel," an old-school term for all the commercials I'd written. See #5, New Freedom Maxi Pads, "Russian," that had been crafted into an animatic (yet another old-school term in the days when Madison Avenue was still a thing).

1987. The When Harry Met Sally *Meg Ryan.*

Malkovich Mash-up

The year was 1987. I was on a flight to New York's JFK from Chicago. I don't remember why I was in Chi-town, but I suspect it was for work. It was probably a meeting about those potty-training baby diapers, Pull-Ups. I believe I'd connected in Chicago to go to Neenah, Wisconsin, where I attended focus groups at the client's headquarters. Now I was headed back home to Manhattan.

I'd worked on this product for an entire year at Ogilvy & Mather, and during it, had the distinct pleasure of rewriting the jingle that went:

"I'm a big kid, look what I can do. I can wear big-kid pants too ... and I can take them up and down ..."

Jaunty musical interlude: Ba da da da dah.

"I'm a big kid NOW."

There was much concern from the client if, when we were saying "up and down," we were encouraging children to take their training pants OFF—to become little exhibitionists, rip off their Pull-Ups, and run around the freezer section of Piggly Wiggly nude, *higgledy piggledy.*

Dizzying amounts of money was spent researching this nugget, this insight. We tested "up and ON" and "up and OFF" to assuage the unhappy mommies that had written in; the winner was the former: "up and ON." Whew, what a relief. Now perhaps the nastygrams the client was receiving would cease.

Anyway, I was sitting in coach (of course) when I learned somehow from some flight attendant murmurings that we had a celebrity on board in first class: Mr. John Malkovich.

Immediately, I was titillated.

I fantasized that he was returning from a play rehearsal at the famed Steppenwolf Theater. Was he Hamlet? Romeo? Just who was he? What was he doing there?

To calm my racing thoughts, I summoned the flight attendant and ordered a little mini bottle of chardonnay. How fitting, I thought, in light of the film, *Being John Malkovich*, during which there was one (or many, can't remember) low ceilings and therefore, everything was small, miniature.

Perhaps that would be my icebreaker when I met him. I'd comment about the irony of this. Better yet, I would send him a note that summarized my observation attached to my diminutive bottle of chardonnay. *Nah. Strike that.*

I sipped my mini chardy all the way back to JFK. I couldn't come up with anything that I felt comfortable saying to him. Plus, I was kind of scared. I didn't want to ask for his autograph. Too normal.

I'd seen him in *Burn This* on Broadway. As we know, he's bald, or near bald with a little top fuzz.

But in the show, he wore a wig, kind of a brunette page boy without bangs. He whooshed his locks around with great abandon like a wild stallion galloping around the stage. Plus, he had a sexy ciggie in hand.

I was spellbound by his performance. He was seductive. Handsome. And oh-so-witty, thanks to the brilliant playwright, Lanford Wilson.

After we landed and deplaned, I figured I'd just see him at the baggage claim and admire him from afar.

As I stood at the carousel, there was no sign of him. Perhaps the John Malkovich Squad had grabbed him, put a brown paper bag over his head to quell/avert the excitement, and tucked him into a limo.

I was kind of sad that I didn't have a celebrity sighting. But figured, hey, no biggie. Life goes on.

My standard, overpacked, giant suitcase on the carousel crept toward me. It was a massive black heap with strange bulges all over it. I could've been smuggling in a small, Pull-Ups wearing child. And I was on the front row so I could grab it, hoist it up, and then head toward the cab stand.

I grabbed my big lug-of-a-bag and gave a heave-ho. But in fear of not being able to lift it, combined with a sudden adrenaline rush, it came flying off at warp speed, and as I whirled it around, there he was: John Malkovich.

But I just didn't whirl it around. My bag (the size of a cruise trunk) came whipping around violently, with a purpose, and within an inch of clipping him at the knees.

I could imagine him being hit, breaking his kneecaps, the EMTs rushing in, the sirens, the flashing lights.

But he then looked at me, his mouth struggling not to laugh. "Can I help you with your bag?" His hand reached out and neared mine on the handle—I had a death grip on it. Then his hand grazed the top of my hand. It softly tickled the top of my knuckles.

Faint. Swoon. Tingles. Fireworks unfolded inside me. (I think I even peed my pants a wee bit. Where were my Pull-Ups?)

"Oh," I said. "No thanks. I've got it." *What was I thinking?* "I'm okay, just a crazy Texas girl who overpacked."

Then I launched into a torrential verbal vomit.

"I saw you read at St. Bart's Episcopal the day that the *Challenger* went down. You read *Franny and Zooey*, by Salinger. I use a quote from his book in the play I am writing, and I quote—from the book, not my play, I want to be clear—so here's the quote, 'I wish I had the courage to be a nobody.'

Franny says this to Zooey when she is wrestling with being rejected from her auditions, she wants to be an actress, you know, have you read the book in its entirety? I just love it. She's so existential, wild and *so me*. Oh, and then you read *Endless Love* by Scott Spencer, and it was so wonderful, much better than the film. Did you see the film *Endless Love*?"

After this stream of my nervosa descended upon him, there was a pause, the kind that's seconds but feels like eons.

Darn it if he didn't smile. His sleepy, sexy eyes smiled, too.

"That is so nice of you to remember. That was quite a day with the *Challenger* going down."

John Malkovich said *going down*.

I could not look at his face, my untethered mind awash with bawdy images.

The entire time we spoke, I kept moving, baby-stepping in kitten heels as I hauled my suitcase. He didn't offer to carry it again, as I did my best to look un-needy, un-weak, you know, not so girly.

He then said, "Would you like to—"

At which point, I was so nervous, I interrupted him. "Okay, so nice meeting you ... buh-bye!!" And off I limped toward the cab stand and back to my lonely life in Manhattan.

In retrospect, I fantasized that he was going to ask me to share a cab into the city, which would of course lead to an affair (wasn't sure if he was married or in between liaisons or he, himself, having an illicit affair with some other star).

The thought was intoxicating.

But the affair would end with my getting ditched, crushed in his palm like a used coffee cup, and thrown in the trash with all the others who dared to canoodle with Mr. Malkovich.

What's a girl to do?

A few weeks later, he opened in a new play on Broadway. I wrote him a letter (phone number included) reminding him of what happened, when, and where, and ... could I buy him a drink?

I took it to the stage door and gave it to some stage hand.

For days, and weeks, I jumped every time my phone rang. Every time I got home, and my message machine light was blinking, I knew it was him.

Remember, this was back in the olden days before anything—cell phone, laptop, social media. No Facebook or Zoom. No Instagram. *Nada.* My only source of contact was my home phone and answering machine.

He never called. But of course, he wouldn't.

I had run away from him. Or this is what I like to think, humoring myself.

Now when I see him in films, I remember that day, his coy smile, and his hand lightly touching mine.

For a moment, there was magic, the kind of stuff that on most days makes me feel all warm and mushy inside, and when I am sad or depressed, electrically alive.

Then I think of peeing in my Pull-Ups. And I am complete.

1993. The Wavy Gillian Anderson with Bangs from The X-Files.

Devo-lution

Mutato. This is the word I think of when I think of Devo. You see, the word "mutato," according to lead singer Mark Mothersbaugh, is a mash up of "mutant" and "potato." Portmanteau, anyone? "Mutato" is also the first part of the moniker for Devo's commercial music venture, Mutato Muzika, and is the very place that I came to work with this epic band.

But this wasn't the first time we'd collaborated. I actually went to Mark's house in the Hollywood Hills, and we composed a song together on his keyboard for a men's suit sale. But that's another story.

The year: 1998. The project: the JCPenney Holiday Campaign. The client had selected fifteen "hot gifts" (read: cheap/affordable) that ranged from generic, slightly festive teddy bears to mini colorful TVs (yellow, pink, blue—they were cute as buttons) to somewhat okay sweaters in mostly unnatural, scratchy blends. We decided that for the maximum media punch each should be :15 and run back-to-back. The consumer would get a quick flurry and assault of cool stuff they just couldn't live without.

Some spots were live action; we shot with Robb Pritts from Backyard Productions. Some required more complicated shoots, so we worked with

Rhythm and Hues, the company famous for the Coca Cola polar bears and the film *Babe: Pig in the City*. We looked at a few music companies to work with but decided that Mutato Muzika was "The One." I mean, who could pass up the opportunity to work with Devo? We knew they'd *whip it good.*

The tracks were always done after the shoots and after the editing. So, when we traipsed into Mutato, we pretty much had the final product. Each :15 spot required a different musical approach. If my memory serves me, (and it usually doesn't, so apologies will abound after this), different teams were responsible for each of the spots. My art director, James, and I worked on a number of them.

But the one in particular that stands head and shoulders above (the sheep, that is), was the spot for wooly sweaters. (Sheep don't have shoulders, but I couldn't resist.) The concept was simple. The sweaters, each with wintery, earthy tones, and crazy patterns, were from sheep who had grown these unique patterns on their fuzzy, woolen bodies—as if the pattern was in their DNA. It was as if JCPenney found these mutant (a theme!) sheep, shaved them, then turned their little patterned coat into sweaters.

The sweater sheep.

It was the late '90s and the whole production took many days involving green screen, layers, lots of post work, and yes, live sheep. The idea was that the sheep would cross in front of the camera. Problem was that the mama sheep wouldn't budge. Only when we positioned their babies on the opposite side of the set would they come a runnin'. And when they'd come a runnin', they each left a trail of nice poopy pellets behind. The PAs would run after them with a shovel scooping up their smelly trail, thus their moniker (instead of Production Assistants): "Poop Assistants."

As was the practice, we'd have a conference call with the music guys/gals before the production, give them ideas about music, the direction, the vibe, then after the shoot, gather to hear the track played against the rough cut.

For some reason, we didn't do this with the Devo dudes. We all showed up at their Sunset Boulevard address without a plan; at least, this was the case with the sheep spot. The building was decidedly, *mutantly* cool, as it was a round building from the '50s that used to be a bank, a solid, green orb, which was painted Mutato green.

We all filed into the workroom. At the helm was Bob Mothersbaugh, Mark's brother. He sat in the engineer's chair at the sound board tapping away, moving buttons, doing all the mysterious things that sound guys do. Above him was the monitor.

James and I sat down on the comfy couch. It was just the three of us, and our producer. There we sat, enduring the silence and waiting for Bob to spin around from his perch (his chair and board were elevated a tad) and talk to us. After the typical intros, requisite questions and discussion of where we'd lunched and where we might dine later, we started discussing music for the spots. The wooly sweater commercial came up and unlike the others prior, we were kinda stuck. We tossed around a couple of ideas, then decided to look at the spot one more time in hopes that it would jog loose a crumb of something.

Then, it happened. Deep from the recesses of my childhood came a melody from my soul, one that I could not *not* share. And just like Old Faithful erupting at Yellowstone, I, too, erupted with the song, singing at the tippy top of my lungs:

“Have you eeeever seen a lassie go this way and that way … have you eeeever seen a lassie go this way and that … go THIS way and THAT way, go THIS way and THAT way … have you eeeever seen a lassie go this way and THAT.”

The look of shock on everyone’s face was as if I had just stood up, pulled up my shirt and revealed my bare teats. Luckily, at that very point, in walked my salvation: Mark Mothersbaugh. The head guy. The one with taste. The one who knew that I had hit upon something. He asked me to sing it again … and again, I sang.

I could then see the uncomfortable looks on my colleagues’ faces transitioning to that of delight, their heads bobbing “yes” to one another. (I’m so glad no one high-fived.) Mark, Bob, and our team continued to discuss what instruments, and then, before we knew it, Mark brought out his accordion. As if he were atop a mountain replete in Tyrolean splendor clad in lederhosen, he played the tune again sans my lyrics or singing. The accordion breathed, expanded, and contracted like a lung—it was alive! We all watched in amazement as Mark cranked out this simple, yet terribly peppy tune on his giant squeeze box.

Beaming, we all heaved a collective sigh of relief.

But it wasn’t over. As I was walking out the door to go to the ladies’ room, I sensed a presence behind me. It was Mark. While I walked down the circular hallway that wrapped around the building, I felt Mark’s hand clasp mine. Then we started skipping together, hand-in-hand, down the hallway, laughing and giggling about the childhood song I had birthed from my memory and heaved out. “Skip, skip, skip to my loo, my darling,” is the refrain we sang. We skipped nearly all the way around the building … and then our hands drifted apart, and we laughingly separated.

Cut to the next day. We’d sent the tracks to the agency to get approval before we did any more work, any polishing. We gathered once more in the room with Bob and Mark. We cued the tracks and played several of them on the speaker phone so our Dallas crew could hear them. The response for all of them was resoundingly enthusiastic, especially the sheep spot. But one track just wasn't doing it for the agency folks.

When Mark heard the lack of love for one track, I could tell he was rattled. After we hung up the phone, Mark said with a sullen, sad face, "I've got to stop hurting people. I've got to get back in therapy."

I could not believe what I was hearing. Mark actually cared what his clients thought, so much so that he felt personally responsible for their reaction. The fact that he shared his need to go back into therapy, the transparency he displayed, broke my heart.

In my ten-year stint working with a large number of musicians in commercial houses, I never thought any of the people cared to this extent. I could be wrong about my assessment. I hope I am. Nor during this decade had I ever met someone so willing to be vulnerable. Indeed, he was an artist of the highest caliber. A fine, dear man.

Mark, superstar that he was, didn't put himself above others. He didn't think himself a god, like so many rock stars do. Despite what the band's name represented, which was the DEVOlution of society, Mark had actually done the opposite—he'd evolved from the disposition that some rock stars possess: egos with their own zip code.

Mark's demeanor, his soul, was so refreshing and startling. Just so cool. The other very cool thing about working with them is that we all walked away with swag: Mutato Muzika knee socks with each word stacked vertically on each sock so that you would read "Mutato" on one side and "Muzika" on the other. Better still, we snagged some "handsome man" hats! These were black, plastic skull caps a la superheroes' slick-black hair. I could almost tuck all my hair underneath it. What a kick they were.

These days, when I hear "Whip It" or any other Devo song, I am reminded of Mark, his lack of egoism, and kindness. In honor of that fanciful day with him, when I hear this song, I, without fail, seem to always get just a little more bounce, a little more skip in my step and *whip it good.*

"Handsome Man" hat given to me by Mark Mothersbaugh, lead singer of Devo.

Their iconic logo.

1998. The Mary Tyler Moore Side-Part Flip.

A Cranston Christmas

When you work on ads for a retail company, your seasons are always all mixed up. Like crazy mixed up. During the spring we were writing ads for fall. During the summer, we were creating campaigns for Christmas. And in the fall, we were concepting for spring. The marketing circle of life.

One August, on our Hollywood soundstage, everything, everywhere was freakin' Christmas. Fluffy green plastic trees decked with festive shiny balls, frosty snowflakes on the walls. Fleecy white tree skirts hugging the tree bases, red and green bows on large boxes that adorned the room. Even some scary elves. These sinister miniatures with pointy hats were positioned in nooks in store shelving we'd created, next to the unsightly patterned sweaters, patterns that were akin to a tornado or at the very least, pizza upchuck.

We endured all this prep and production in record heat. Some days got up to 108. So, in Cali, where we did all our work, it wasn't just hot, it was Death Valley hot. One shoot was especially insufferable. We were in the desert handling sweaters and corduroy jumpers for a back-to-school sale. We got so sweaty and haggard that we looked like we'd all been out changing a flat on our scouting van.

Finally, we decided that we'd had enough of near heat strokes, sweaty pits, and smeared mascara running down our collective cheeks. We decided to shoot in the store. This meant that we would have to shoot inside an actual store, but after business hours—we'd start shooting at 9 p.m. and break at dawn.

Prior to our LA shoot, during the "concepting" phase at the agency, we usually got together to write the script in a cluster. And we all had positions. There was Mr. Beginning, Mr. Middle, and Mr. Ending (this was the classic structure of a :30 spot.) I didn't care if I was called a mister. In this group, being a mister was an honor. I'm creatively gender-fluid.

As per usual, we all gathered in one of our very brown, dull conference rooms, cranked out a script quickly then spent even more time trying to figure out where we'd go for lunch.

We then took it to the client, presented it, and bing, bang, boom, it was approved.

We shot all of our spots in LA. In fact, we *had* to go to LA, as our big boss (head honcho guy) saw something that we'd shot locally, was horrified because the film was so sub-par, and demanded that we not do this again. We didn't.

So off we jetted to the City of Angels to prep.

We hired a very hip, very glittery Hollywood-y couple, who were married, and who had names that went together, kind of like Bogie and Bacall, but not Bogie and Bacall. I think they had one name that was a mash-up of their names, like Nancy Michael or Bennifer. Something that rolled off the tongue, and a name I'm sure our client (God love him) could drop when he was picking up girls at Champs.

The Man Director had a shock of black curly hair and a goatee, way before it was The Thing to Grow. The Woman Director was slim, brunette, sexy, and interesting—*not* a Barbie doll.

A few days before the shoot in LA we did our casting. We needed someone funny. We would've loved to get a famous comedian. At the time, Seinfeld was *it*. THE guy to hire. Could we get Jerry Seinfeld? Uh, no. But we could dream.

What about Carrot Top, someone asked?

No. Too frightening. We would get slammed with customer letters for sure. Plus, my art director had a fear of redheads, you know, ginger people. He thought they were from the devil. But then we hit upon an idea: If we can't get Jerry Seinfeld, what about someone who was on *Seinfeld*?

Enter Bryan Cranston, Elaine's re-gifting dentist boyfriend.

The day of the shoot arrived and for some reason, I was the only writer on the set along with my brilliant boss, Glenn. There I was, all self-important and smiling about the script—all our witticisms, turns of phrases, and so on that we'd birthed.

In walked Bryan. He was handsome. Cute handsome. Cute boyish handsome with dimples that grabbed my heart and yanked it out of my chest.

He examined the script, read it to himself, musing (I thought) over the clever monologue he was to deliver.

In the spot, we had a series of things that Bryan was to interact with as he made his way through the store ostensibly Christmas shopping: old man jeans, jewelry (teeny tiny chip diamond stuff), perfume, stuffed animal puppet-y things called Pillow Pets, and finally, roller luggage.

For the last scene, he had to deliver a line, "I got in, I got out. Nobody got hurt." Bryan gave us oodles of takes. All good, all different. But they just weren't what I had in my mind.

I stood back and let the directors do their work, but not without yammering in Glenn's ear (best boss ever) about this one last take. He, who was accustomed to (God bless him) putting up with my crapola, calmly told me to hang tight, that "we'd get it." But I could see he was irritated.

I finally walked up to the directors and gave them a line reading.

"You know, it needs to be more ... more ... offhanded ... casual ... no, I mean, it needs to be more ... proud ..." On I went. What I wanted to say was that it needed to sound like me. But how would I tell them this?

The Woman of the Man-Woman team gave him the line reading, and my skin started to itch. It was *so not* the way I had said it. It needed to be funny. She was not funny.

But since they were being paid thousands each for their day rate, I clinched my hands and gave a Charlie Brown smile.

Again, Bryan delivered the line, "I got in, I got out, nobody got hurt."

By this time, I *wanted* to hurt someone.

The Man of the Man-Woman team looked at me. He turned from his director's chair and gave me a thumbs up, as in, "Do we have it?"

I crept closer to the directors' chairs, stood right behind them, and asked him if we could give it another go.

I could see that Bryan was growing weary. So again, nice guy that he was, he did it again.

Still, it was not *exactly* what I had in mind.

I got a look from one of the frustrated directors and heard, "Lisa, why don't you give him a line reading?"

I was already overstepping my bounds and awkwardly lodged between their two spindly-legged canvas chairs. When I heard this, I made a beeline for Bryan, jostling them each a bit when I busted through with my child-bearing hips.

Trying to be coy and flirty, tense as I was because the clock was ticking (and I could see the crew giving me a lot of eye rolls and frowny faces), I gave him the line reading. I inched close to his face and said, over-articulating, "I got in, I got out, nobody got hurt." He looked at me. I looked at him. We connected.

The heavens parted. He did the line. It was perfect. And prince of a guy that he was, he kept on repeating the line a few more times just the way I liked it, just for grins.

The directors called "cut" and it was a wrap. I'd gotten my way-too-important line reading.

The truth is that he made each scenario in our TV spot leagues funnier than it had originally been scripted, just by being himself.

After the shoot, he and I got a Polaroid together. I cherish it, as it shows my younger, thinner (brunette) self, and him with more hair.

On our JCPenney set in Hollywood.

Cut to many years later. I knew Bryan had landed the dad role in *Malcolm in the Middle*, which tickled me. But when he became Walter White in *Breaking Bad*, I was elated.

Unlike his comedic role on *Seinfeld* and in our TV spot, what emerged in Walter was this genius actor who revealed his true talents to the world. I hung on every episode and stayed up until the wee hours binge-watching, unable to tear myself away from each gripping, cliffhanging, meth-addled story. I was an addict.

His career had more than exploded; I felt really lucky and humbled to have worked with him.

Looking back, I'm embarrassed of my hubris—me, the average-Jane copywriter giving the lauded Bryan Cranston a line reading. When I think back on his humility and good humor, I'm gobsmacked with gratitude.

These days, every time I see him on the big screen, I'm *breaking happy* each and every time.

2004. The Jennifer Lopez Updo (in my Dreams).

Julie Newmar: Real-Life Superhero

A few years ago, over a Labor Day weekend, I was visiting some old friends in Los Angeles. I decided to treat myself, as well as indulge in a little bittersweet remembrance of times past when I was lucky enough to have a per diem, where I wined and dined on the company dime in the '90s. I booked a room at the very green and white, posh hotel, the Viceroy, with interiors by Kelly Wearstler, international style icon, whose palette boasted dreamy, verdant colors that popped amidst travertine-hued neutrals.

However, the only wrinkle was, well, *wrinkles.*

Mine.

Those facial lines and crow's feet that I could not escape seeing when I was there. On every bedroom wall there was a collage of mirrors. Big mirrors. Inches apart.

Everywhere I turned, I was faced with myself. The good, the bad, and the ugly. I decided to not make eye contact with myself but look down at the carpet when walking about the room. I got dizzy doing this and gave up after a while. What I saw was what I got.

One night, when I returned from dinner, I walked up and there was a long snaky line out front that was topped off with a doorman and the despotic velveteen rope. I say "despotic" because in New York when club hopping, especially during winter, unless you were a super model (not me), a movie star (not me), or on the list (not me), you shivered out in the cold in blustery winds until you either miraculously got picked, tailed in after someone, or gave up and decided to go to an old, broken-down, has-been club like Danceteria got to be in the '80s, ashamed and defeated, and sipped on watered-down Manhattans.

I had a visceral reaction when I saw this human impediment—a shame-laced flashback struck my gut. Luckily, I was a party guest. I was not only *on* the list, but I was also sleeping at the hotel. So, I walked right up in front of everyone, flashed my room key and waltzed right in. Liberation, at last.

The party was at the pool, a coveted area that glistened in style and populace. The hotties were out tonight. The area was swimming in tanned legs and spindly tall heels, upon which gazelles teetered when they hobbled past. Guys with hipster stubble and matching baldish, fuzzy heads sunglass-clad (at night) slunk by. Some wore hats, pork pie hats a la John Lurie in *Stranger Than Paradise.*

I don't do hats. I can't. I look like an egghead, and I feel like Marty Feldman, my eyes always wide with fear and awkwardness about said hat I am trying to pull off.

This night, I wore no hat or any Daisy Dukes or anything remotely revealing. In fact, I wore jean shorts to my knees, jorts. And mules. I baby-stepped my way down to the pool. I don't walk too well in backless shoes—been known to topple over and sprain my ankle on occasion. I wasn't taking any chances.

I positioned myself on a little tree stump. It probably wasn't a stump, but it felt like one, it was so uncomfortable. I was about butt height to all who passed me, so it was an odd vantage point. But I liked it. I felt safe. I could sit here, inhale the electricity and dynamic of the night while gazing at the soft, blue waters of the pool. The palm trees, tall as skyscrapers, added a nice ceiling to the evening.

Then he appeared. A man, dressed in white linen from head to toe. He was tanned, too. But thankfully, not like George Hamilton.

He asked if he could join me.

"Of course," I said.

As soon as he sat down, he started talking. We exchanged the usual pleasantries like name, where are you from, what are you doing here, etc. Turns out this man was a lawyer. On and on we chatted about everything and nothing. Somehow, he asked me if I wanted to go workout with him tomorrow at Ryan O'Neal's gym.

What was I hearing? Seriously? As if I would be seen in a leotard exposing my extra 30-pounds-since-college body to the starry Ken doll beau of *Love Story*? Getting into certain undignified and highly awkward workout poses, some spread eagle? In my mind, I screamed, "NO WAY!"

As if by a will of its own, my mouth spoke the words, "Why, YES, I'd love to!"

I diminished my responses, *oh-sure-right*, yawned, then excused myself. Told him I needed to get some rest for tomorrow morning. We exchanged vital contact info and off I went.

As I walked away, I was still reeling from my decision, what my renegade mouth had said.

That night, I didn't sleep very well, obsessed about the morning. But I made one big decision: I would wear a butt wrap with my leotard. You know, a SOFA, Sweater Over Fat Ass. An appropriate camouflage. I wouldn't get into any machine (inner thigh) that required me to spread my legs like at the gyno.

What would I say if I was introduced to him? And what about makeup? Without it, I have no eyebrows. I looked very Elizabethan. I decided I'd wear brown eyebrow pencil. I had to.

My mind, on a loop, didn't calm down until around 2 a.m.

I awoke with a start and popped out of bed waiting for my friend to call. I ordered breakfast. Then I looked out my window—well, no, I craned my neck to see the ocean view I had been promised. There were big, busy streets between the hotel and the Pacific ... then there was a good chunk of buildings, *then* the ocean. If I looked carefully, I could see a bit of it, but "a bit" was better than none, coming from landlocked, concrete Dallas.

I dawdled around a bit more. Still no call. Heart thumping, I called him. Turns out he had stayed up a bit late, or that is what I heard in his gravelly voice. He asked if we could go to Ryan's gym the next day. WHAT? I had wrung my hands and thoughts for no good reason? Lost sleep?

I was not happy. But I agreed to his offer to grab a burger at a diner. With all the outdoor places to sit in the sun, I was not crazy about doing this, but I went with it.

The diner was in Brentwood, much like an old Hollywood place that Lucy and Ricky might have frequented. He had his burger. I had my soggy, sad, iceberg-lettuce-infested chef salad. To complete the Lucy/Ricky scenario, I ordered a hot cup of black coffee to go with my greens.

"You know, there is someone I'd like to introduce you to, a friend of mine," he said.

"Who would that be?"

"Julie Newmar."

I had heard the name but couldn't immediately place her.

"Catwoman, the original Catwoman. I've done some work for her and she's really a great person."

This was finally getting interesting. An old school superhero. I was psyched.

Let's go!

Julie's house was near the diner. Off we sped through the winding streets of Brentwood. When we arrived, he drove up the driveway, all the way to the back. The house was California-chic and as those houses go, smallish and deceptively expensive.

We walked in through sliding glass doors. There she was: Julie Newmar.

She stood and fed a young adult man who was seated at the table. He had some sort of disability. Down Syndrome, perhaps.

She glowed. Her face, her hair, her smile. All glowing. She was very, very thin, a former dancer. We all said "hello," then she introduced me to her son, who she said was deaf. At that moment, I was obviously struck deaf because I said to her son, "Hi John," at which point, both my friend and Julie in unison said, "HE'S DEAF."

I shrunk a foot. My mouth had a mind of its own yet again. My friend told me that Julie had John when she was around fifty. Since then, he said she had been a selfless, dedicated mother.

As she talked, she delicately, lovingly lifted spoonful after spoonful of food into her sweet son's mouth. He had rich, chestnut hair, and doleful big eyes. I was touched by her composure and unflinching grace. She kind of purred.

She gave us a tour around her house. It was marvelous. Tasteful in design and decoration. She even gave us a tour of the backyard and told us about a feud she had with her neighbor, Jim Belushi, concerning a fence. I am not sure of the details, but it was pretty brutal. She talked about it with passion and fervor. I could see a bit of her claws coming out, but they quickly retracted.

She was alive and moving fast. It was hard keeping up with her as she scampered around her property.

I believe at the time she was close to eighty years old.

When I got close to her face, it was shining and flawless. My friend said she hadn't had any work done. No cosmetic surgery. Nothing.

I believed him.

In her heyday, she was an exotically gorgeous dancer, singer, and actress, the daughter of a Ziegfeld Follies performer. Her career had been magical, kissed by fate at every turn. (There was even the movie *Too Wong Foo, Thanks for Everything! Julie Newmar,* that she did later, but one I never saw nor had any desire to—really bad title.) Well, now, I don't ever have to see that film because I have met the real thing!

Julie Newmar was beautiful as when I met her as she was when she was Catwoman.

But she was leagues more beautiful to me now. Her adoration and care for her son shone brighter than her outer physical God-given features. To me, she really was a superhero. A woman, a mother who loved her son unabashedly, a mother who would undoubtedly take a bullet for him.

The juxtaposition between Julie's physical perfection and her son's handicap ripped my heart right out of my chest. Her son's seemingly compromised life seemed so unfair. But life, as we well know is, decidedly and often, unfair.

Once she was leaping across rooftops in Gotham. When I met her, she was gently depositing food into her deaf son's mouth, nourishing, I'm sure, his soul as much as his body.

I was blessed to have met you, Julie Newmar, especially now that you're in your role of a lifetime.

You may have played an anti-hero, but to me, you are, indeed, a real-live superhero.

2000. The Auburn Andie MacDowell.

Crowe's Feet

In 2000, I was in LA on a job. I was producing a radio spot I had written for JCPenney. At the time, my mother was in the Russell Crowe fan club. She and her friends, both in the Crowe's Nest and the Silver Crowes, were agog about all things Russell: his latest movie; where he was filming; who he was dating (sleeping with); where he was last spotted; who he was with; and I'm sure, what he had for breakfast and if it gave him gas.

She and I had traveled to Austin a number of times to see his band, TOFOG, perform. TOFOG is an acronym for a film term: Twenty Odd Foot of Grunts. As opposed to laughs, or snorts, or farts.

Laminated, wallet-sized memento.

During my trip to LA, she suggested I contact some fans, as there was a party where TOFOG was playing that they were going to that I *had* to attend. It was a wrap party for the movie, *Mystery, Alaska,* starring Russell and Judith Ivey. It was at the Viper Room, the place where River Phoenix died of an overdose.

I didn't know any of Mom's friends. They were all sizes, shapes, and ages: gray hair retiree; tall, blond, gorgeous dentist and aspiring actress; another had tattoos up and down each arm, totally sleeved out and wore overalls and a t-shirt to display her body artwork and her pitiable endured pain; and one woman from Brooklyn who was rumored to be an email pal of Russell's.

Prior to the fete, we decided to meet for dinner, then go to the Viper Room, where we were on *The List.* It wasn't dark yet, perhaps around 6 p.m. We arrived with a clatter, the sundry crew that we were. In front of the door was an enormous, round, and slightly balding gentleman the size of a bus. He wore a black suit, white shirt, and shades. He did not smile and was giving *Sopranos* vibes.

Up walked one of us, the tall, blond dentist/actress. She had pretty, white teeth and was oh-so lovely, so we thought she was our best candidate to approach this formidable wall of a human.

They exchanged pleasantries and then, the velvet rope was lifted, and we were in. Inside, the joint looked like a '40s nightclub. Red leather booths ringed the room. Atop some of these sat white, crisp name cards that read "Reserved." There were a few tables in the middle and on one wall, the stage where TOFOG would play.

En masse, we moved toward the bar to get our adult beverages. I ordered the house white wine. The others indulged in stronger fare: vodka, tequila, and whiskey. The lights were dim and moody, except for the wall of bright, white light behind the liquor bottles that were on shelves behind the bar. An EDM track purred as we crept around the club.

The crowd was thin: guys with hipster dark hair, goatees, soul patches, in worn sexy jeans; a few older guys with gray beards who looked like they might be electricians, gaffers, etc.; beautiful young women in revealing, boob-a-licious outfits who milled around, and emitted squeals followed by too-long hugs and air kisses for everyone.

We had trouble finding a table, as they were all reserved, so we decided to assume a position at the back of the room.

Then it happened. The buzz. The whispering. The gasps. Russell Crowe was in the house.

With lots of craning of necks and subtle (and not-so-subtle) pointing, we located him.

His hair was wild and woolly. He wore a navy-blue shirt and jeans. Nothing special.

It was at this point that I felt it—the urge to go up and meet him. My mother had been so nuts about him. Every conversation ended up being about Russell. As I said, "All roads lead to Russell with Mom these days."

I had an obligation. I threw back a big gulp of the glaringly average chardonnay. And made my approach. I tapped him on the shoulder. "Hi, are you Russell?" Looking back, I am awed at my talent for stating the obvious.

"What's your name?"

"Lisa." My voice, a shaky whisper. "My mother is huge fan, so I just had to come over and meet you and shake your hand."

His eyes were blue, stained-glass windows, a kaleidoscope of sky blue and deep azure. His Aussie accent was thick, as was his five o'clock shadow. "You tell your mum hello for me."

I became lightheaded, short of breath. The awkward silence was bellowing. We were face to face, locked in a gaze that was heavy with interest from my side and perceived slight interest (mine) from his side. At that point, I just slid my hand out of his manly grasp and stepped back. That was it.

I ran back, breathless, aflutter, exhilarated. I was a mini celebrity within my group. The questions came forth in a blazed fury: What were his eyes like? How did his skin feel? How close were you to his face? How did he smell?

TOFOG was slated to play in about a half hour, so we refueled with a variety of spirits: gin, vodka, whiskey. And of course, my mediocre, quite un-buttery vino.

The place filled up pretty quickly around showtime. We scanned the crowd looking for Danny DeVito and Kim Basinger at those hallowed reserved tables. I did get a glimpse of the shine atop Danny's cue ball, bald head. Kim was nowhere to be seen.

Then the lights dimmed. The crowd cheered. Russell and band were about to hit the stage. The velvet curtains opened. Drums clattered, and guitars wailed. A veil of starstruck-ness fell upon the room, all of us sporting our "O" face.

All eyes were on Russell.

Our valiant group managed to work our way through the masses and were positioned on the front row. I was just left of the microphone and pressed boob-height against the stage. My wine glass sat precariously, threatening to tip over, at the very edge.

TOFOG started their set with an all-time favorite, one with jaunty, jangly guitars and lyrics about crossing a river. Russell then sang about heartbreak, lost love, each with a pained look, expressed through his eyebrows and furrowed forehead a la James Dean.

I'd thrown back a few more chardonnays, so I was feeling a bit daring, even more so than I'd been when I met Russell.

I was eye-level with the stage and Russell's feet. They were bare. I noticed the hair on his toes. They were so tempting, so cute, like little pink (albeit hairy) shrimps right in a row. As if I was possessed with some foreign spirit, all reason escaping me, I reached out and grabbed his toes.

Without flinching, he yanked his foot from my grasp and launched into another song. Then, he looked at me—and winked. I let out a "yahoo" like a shrieking wildebeest. I'd been validated. I existed. I was not invisible.

Why was this so important? Why did I need a celebrity to validate my existence? My take on this: We hold up celebrities in our society as modern-day gods from Greek society who possess immortality and superpowers. We don't want to be nobodies. We want to matter. We want to be loved.

If we are approved of by this lot, then somehow, we, too, become elevated from the masses. And for a brief moment, we shine.

When the concert was over (and after two encores), the band escaped out a side door. Our group rushed as fast as we could through the cloggy mob after them to beg for autographs. One even went out the front and around to the side to see if she could see The Man, or better still, snag a band member.

But they'd vanished. Rumor was they were staying at the Bel-age (nicknamed the "Gar-baahge" by my former ad world colleagues) so we got the bright idea to go in search of them at the hotel. We snuck in and took to the stairwells, yelling their names, opening doors on each floor to see if any heads popped out of any doors. I'm surprised we weren't arrested. This continued for a while until we gave up. No such luck. It was time to go back to our hotel.

That was over a decade ago. Since then, Russell has won an Oscar, had two kids, and got a divorce. And until his starring role in *Noah*, (a far cry from the young, strapping gladiator years earlier), he has seemingly slipped from Hollywood's radar.

How quickly one can disappear, like a vapor, from the limelight. How fickle the studios can be. I wonder if Russell ever felt invisible during those days of non-screen time? The last pic I saw of Russell reflected an older, grayer man. The man whose foot I grabbed, now had, yes, crow's feet. Time can be cruel to the beautiful. Happily, though, my memory of meeting him is not tarnished. Both of us, he and I, will always be young, less wrinkled, and vibrant, sans sagging, high LDL, or dark circles.

I can safely say this man, Mr. Russell Crowe, and my memory of meeting him that star-filled night, will always bring me to my feet.

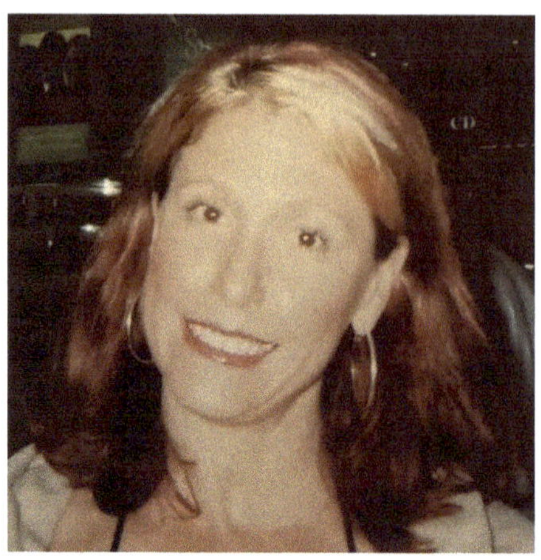

2008. The Cruella De Vil Blond Streak.

Toe to Toe with Patrick

This saga began in Chicago's O'Hare airport in 2008. Mom and I were on our way to London to see her favorite opera star, Bryn Terfel, in *Tosca* at Covent Garden. We were slated to meet a group of people from the fan club, the Terfeliads, a group of women who caravaned around the world to see this dashing Welsh superstar fill their hearts with bass baritone splendor. They are, as I like to say, the Dead Heads of the opera world. We fit right in.

Icy weather delayed us out of Dallas, so we knew we'd have a miniscule window in which to make our connecting flight to the UK. So here we came, down the wide, cavernous, echoing main promenade at O'Hare, running as fast as our nonsensible shoes with spindly, ankle-breaking heels could take us to our gate. We showed up staggering and sweaty, hair flying in every direction (except for Mom's), dragging our overpacked bags behind us like body bags.

Then we saw it: the plane slowly pulling away from the gate.

"Aah!" we both moan, and looked at each other with utter despair, dropping our bags with overly dramatic flair, flinging our arms in the air, saying, "We were sooooo close!" (I don't know why I say "we." I was the only one doing this. Mom was her usual elegant, dignified self.)

With crestfallen hearts, we started wringing our hands and worrying about what we might do next. How would we make it to see Bryn?

As we were doing this, I noticed a man to our left. He, too, had missed the connecting flight and was less than enthused. He mentioned he'd hoofed it all the way from his gate, a flight from LA. Only thing was, he didn't look disheveled or rattled in any way. No hairs out of place. No sweat around his collar. No, he was hip and cool in his dark leather jacket, toting a black carry-on and interestingly, a giant film reel the size of a dinner plate charger (but thicker) on a small trolley.

He looked familiar, but not immediately so. He was definitely Captain Hunk—tall with dark, distinct eyes, and perfectly arched brows. He had an elfish, mischievous grin. Killer dimples. His voice slayed me, very deep and resonant like an FM radio announcer. I knew he was *somebody*, but I didn't know just *who*.

Mom and I struck up a conversation with this friendly, handsome man. He was out of ideas, too, about how we were going to get to London. We talked to him for a few minutes, sharing our mutual irritations about the plight of air travel while we all droned on, frowning, and fretting.

In a few minutes, an American Airlines gate attendant, in her red-and-blue-scarfed self, appeared and told us we'd be on the next flight. Not to worry. It would depart about midnight, and it would be taking off a few gates away. Soon more people who'd missed their connection arrived, then we all waddled en masse like little ducklings with our bags down to the new gate. Mom and I decided to get some sandwiches for our long flight, so off I went to fetch our nourishment.

When I returned with full bags and sodas from Which Wich, a conversation between Mom, aka The Redheaded Bombshell, (named by a trucker at Piggly Wiggly), and this mystery man with the film reel was in full swing.

"Lisa, this is Patrick Warburton. He's on *Seinfeld. SEINFELD,*" she said in an elevated tone. "He was Puddy, Elaine's boyfriend. He's been in lots of TV shows and movies."

"I thought I recognized you," I said. "I knew you were somebody. Just didn't know which body of the some you were."

He smiled and eked out a courtesy laugh. I asked about his film reel. Turns out he was taking it to the Irish Film Festival in Dublin—he was one of the main stars, Mack. I think the film was *Made for Each Other*. Here's the IMDB plot summary:

The best part of any marriage is consummating it. However, after 3 months of a sexless marriage, Dan finds himself in the throes of casual sex with another woman. Dan decides the only way to morally rectify this is, of course, to get his wife to cheat on him and thus he sets out to find the right man to even the score.

"My daughter, Lisa, she did a film, too," Mom said.

"Yes, your mother was filling me in on your documentary." Patrick seemed to have a glimmer in his eye, as he popped open his Coke can.

My mind was twittering about what else Mom had told him about me while I was away getting our food. Did she tell him I was a spinster who used to write ads in New York but was currently unemployed? Did she tell him I wore corrective shoes as a child? That I hid behind the door when I was a toddler when I had a dirty diaper?

"Yes, I did a film about a homeless guy, Bob, *His Name is Bob*, and the tagline is 'The story of a spiritual savant who survives his own personal holocaust.'" He uttered a witty remark, and I returned with something that was less than witty, I'm sure. But the volley was on.

Mom told Patrick all about Bryn, and gave him Bryn's operatic CV, i.e., where we had gone to see him (New York, Chicago, Houston, etc.), who was in the fan club, and more. He seemed genuinely interested. It came time for us to board, so we continued a bit of conversation as we trudged on and found our seats.

As it turned out, Patrick was sitting right behind me. Not to the left. Not to the right. But directly behind me.

After we got settled and the flight took off, we resumed our volley. He talked about the cast on *Seinfeld*, *The Tick*, as well as *Family Guy*, and the many other characters he voiced in the cartoon world.

I told him I'd written a TV spot for JCPenney in which we cast Bryan Cranston, Elaine's other boyfriend, the dentist re-gifter, on *Seinfeld*.

"He was your competition," I said.

"No contest," he said, indicating that Bryan was clearly the better, more suave of the two.

We continued to chat, then he pulled out his wallet, bragged about his wife and kids, and showed me photos of his progeny—quite a few; he had four. They had his DNA, all gorgeous.

"You are prolific," I said. He blushed.

He told me how hard it was to have a family and be an actor. Was he flirting? Certainly not, I thought. I was a Pleb. He was Hollywood soon-to-be royalty, a patrician. But I did try to empathize with him, telling him that when I was on the road doing TV commercials, I couldn't have pets or plants.

"My plants died. Even my cactus. And I had to give away my lab, my sweet Simon," I said.

He raised his eyebrows a bit, mumbling, "Yeah, I know what you mean."

I'm not sure the parallel was really the same. I was, though, trying.

I shared more about the woes of being a part-time filmmaker but said we did have a track by Tom Waits, whom he said he loved. I dubbed this a personal victory.

Over the course of the six-hour flight, it was a verbal joust. We talked on and off about films, TV, books, music, et al. When I thought of something to say or ask him, I would pop up over the seat and talk to him. He would do the same to me. We were like little whack-a-moles jutting up from each side of our seats. Mom even joined in on our conversation, piping up about movies she liked, even musical groups.

"Even though my first love is Bryn, I really like the Bee Gees," Mom said.

"They are some snappy dressers, those guys. Their white platform shoes alone should be feared," Patrick said. Mom giggled and he winked at her.

Near the end of the flight, we both decided we needed to sleep.

As we started our descent, the flight attendant announced that we'd be landing in about an hour and that we needed to wake up, make sure we did our customs forms, and other blah-blah things we needed to do to enter the country.

Suddenly, I felt something touching my socked-footed feet—Patrick's toes! He was tall enough that he could stick his feet under my seat and tickle my toes with his!

I jumped up, making a big scene, bursting into laughter, and looked up to see him laughing, too.

"Just had to wake you up, make sure we didn't lose you during sleepy time," Patrick said.

After we landed and were gathering our belongings, he said to Mom, "This is for you. I want you to have this." It was a jar of orange hard candies with an orange ribbon on the top. I have no idea where he got these, but he was insistent about parting with them.

Mom gushed.

"You keep an eye on her," Patrick said, nodding his head in the direction of Mom. "You never know what The Redheaded Bombshell is going to do next."

When we deplaned, we said our goodbyes. We wished him well at the Irish Film Festival and with his connecting flight to Dublin.

"You better hurry," Mom said.

“Oh yes, ma’am, I better skedaddle.”

And off he went, with his film on the trolley that clacked and clacked on the marble floor until the sound was just a whisper.

Mom kept the jar of orange candies—unopened. And every time she saw them or him in his commercial for National Car Rental, she told the story: “Do you remember the time was saw Patrick Warburton on the way to London? You know he gave me some candies.”

If I ever saw Patrick Warburton again, I am doubtful he’d remember me. But at least, I’ll always have that moment when we went toe to toe.

2010. The Messy Mimi Rogers.

Mom and the Former First Lady

Mom got her hair "done," as in "done." You know what I mean. She went once a week to the beauty salon where her red hair was washed, curled up in hard, neon-pink curlers, dried under a domed dryer from the 1960s, and then back-combed, all to create a very pretty hair helmet, impervious to everything from a brisk wind to an earthquake.

Her nickname was "The Redheaded Bombshell." It came from an old white-haired, grisly truck driver who shouted out to her, "Well, here comes The Redheaded Bombshell," as she crossed in front of his Mac truck one Sunday afternoon at the Piggly Wiggly.

For her signature style, she went to a salon in Dallas that was tucked away on the ground floor of a '70s-style high rise that was affectionately known as "The Gay 90s." Everyone who lived there was either gay or ninety years old. However, the salon had been in Dallas, at different locations, since the swinging '60s when big hair was big business in this town.

Mom's hairdresser was a woman named Ann who wore gingham checked dresses (mostly red and white) like Loretta Lynn. She also had a parrot named Rambo. Ann liked to imitate Rambo when she was doing Mom's hair. They'd laugh and have a grand old time.

One day, Mom was sitting under the dryer and a woman passed by who looked very familiar to her. "Where do I know her from? I am sure I know her. Maybe she used to be in my Sunday School class years ago down at First Methodist."

Mom walked up, with her hair still in pink curlers, to the woman who was getting a manicure and put her hand on the woman's forearm, as only a Southern belle would do. "Tell me your name."

The woman looked up, smiled ever so graciously. "Laura Bush."

Mom launched in. "Oh, that's right! You were a Kappa Alpha Theta at SMU, right?"

"Why yes I was," said the former First Lady.

"My daughter was a Kappa Alpha Theta at SMU."

"What is her name?"

And she told her my name. And then they smiled. And from what Mom said, she was delightful and lovely. Mom said her hair looked just the same as it did when she was First Lady: discreet, brown, and short. The very picture of elegance.

I found it wonderfully refreshing that Mom asked about her sorority and didn't ask about her international fame, living in the White House, and being First Lady—what was it like dining with the Russian Premier?

Is the White House really haunted?

Is it true you are really a Democrat and used to smoke cigarettes?

Were you near George when that shoe was thrown at him in the Middle East?

Are the Secret Service guys hot?

I later found out that Mrs. Bush went to this salon because she could slip in and out easily. The security risk was low. The Secret Service didn't have to worry about her being out in the wide open among the crazies.

And, just when the Former First Lady was trying to lay low and enjoy her life with George in relative anonymity, here came Mom, The Redheaded

Bombshell, completely busting Mrs. Bush's cover. But, as everyone knew, Mama didn't beat around the bush.

Mom and I at the Staatsoper in Vienna in 2008.

Afterword

It's 2026. Both my parents are gone. I look at my wrinkled skin sometimes and see them reflected in it. There isn't a day I don't think about them, or something—a song, a smell—that reminds me of them. Gratitude is not an adequate expression of how I feel about this. Grief never goes away. It just changes its shape.

The privilege of having John as my witty, intellectual Dad, and Phyllis as my gentle songbird of a Momma, was a precious gift, as well as a bona fide hoot. Our home was filled with so many belly laughs, opera blaring, and Johnson flat feet, but most of all, love.

I'm thankful I grew up the way I did—in a beauty salon. Mamaw was the receptionist. Papaw did the towels. In the evenings, my brothers and I would sweep all the wisps and loose strands from the floor. It was a regular Family Hair Affair.

Though decades prior, I wasn't grateful. I was made fun of because Dad did hair and owned a salon. Further, the tyranny of beauty, of image, was seared into my sinews. But now, I try my hardest to wear the world, and all its fleshly trappings, like a loose garment.

Or rather, a free and easy hairstyle.

Had Mom not gotten off the bus at Ross and Harwood in downtown Dallas—she said a little voice told her to—she wouldn't have met Dad in the choir at First Methodist Church. And I wouldn't have been born, then lived to show up like Forrest Gump in the most unlikely of situations to have my hair brushes with fame.

Lisa Johnson Mitchell's work has appeared in *X-R-A-Y, Fictive Dream,* and *Cleaver,* among others. One of her pieces was a Finalist in the 2022 London Independent Story Prize Competition. Another received First Place in the 2021 *Button Eye Review* Summer Contest and placed in the Top 10 of the 2020 *Columbia Journal* Short Fiction Contest. Other works have been honored by *Glimmer Train*, ScreenCraft, and PEN Women. She was a resident at the Vermont Studio Center and holds an MFA from Bennington College.

www.ingramcontent.com/pod-product-compliance
Lightning Source LLC
LaVergne TN
LVHW052355100826
845147LV00013B/848

9798899904592